## "Sorry about that, Paul,"

Rachel said.

"What?"

"I was just trying to have a little fun. I'm afraid things got a little out of hand and now Maggie and Sara think we're...you know...a couple."

"Yeah. Bummer."

"I'm serious, Paul. You don't know my sisters. By morning they'll have us in a full-blown romance. They're probably peeking out the windows and wondering why you don't kiss me goodnight."

He grinned and stroked her cheek. "Why, Ms. Duke, I thought you'd never ask."

## Books by Anna Schmidt

Love Inspired

*Caroline and the Preacher* #72
*A Mother for Amanda* #109
*The Doctor's Miracle* #146

## ANNA SCHMIDT

has been writing most of her life. Her first "critical" success was a short poem she wrote for a Bible study class in fourth grade. Several years later she launched her career as a published author with a two-act play and several works of nonfiction. This is her twelfth novel, and she hopes one of many more for Steeple Hill.

Anna is a transplanted Virginian, living now in Wisconsin. She works part-time doing public relations for an international company, and enjoys traveling, gardening, long walks in the city or country and antiquing. She is currently at work on a screenplay in addition to developing new story ideas for future novels.

# The Doctor's Miracle
## Anna Schmidt

*Love Inspired*®

Published by Steeple Hill Books™

STEEPLE HILL BOOKS

Steeple
Hill™

ISBN 0-373-87153-8

THE DOCTOR'S MIRACLE

Come, let us cry out with joy to Yahweh,
Acclaim the rock of our salvation.
Let us come into His presence with thanksgiving,
Acclaim Him with music.

—*Psalms* 95:1, 2

**To the healers and the survivors**

# *Chapter One*

Rachel Duke blinked at the lights and smiled at the audience. She took a deep breath. Just one more song and she might win the talent search. Unbelievably, she stood in the midst of a dream coming true. She settled herself onto the high stool a stagehand had placed in front of the microphone and waited for the audience to recover from the rocking fervor of the last performer.

Her last number—the one that had won her the spot as a finalist in the talent search for new faces at the Grand Ole Opry—had been a rousing gospel classic. She had gotten the audience involved, and when she left the stage they had given her a raucous ovation that included cheers and whistles. She could see that they were anticipating something similar, and she hoped her change of pace would not disappoint them.

As she strummed the strings of the guitar to check the pitch and to capture their full attention, she saw Doc McCoy hurrying to the seat she had reserved for him. She nodded in his direction even as she caught sight of the tall, dark, bearded man following him. That would be Doc's son, Paul McCoy.

She had tried to assure Doc that she was fine on her own and there was no need for him to be there, but he had insisted.

"I'm not about to miss your big night, Rachel," he had announced. Doc had served as surrogate father for Rachel and her siblings ever since their parents had died when Rachel was twelve.

"Doc, Paul will be exhausted. It must take hours to fly from Kosovo, not to mention the connections and delays. He's going to be anxious to get home."

"He's young," Doc had replied cheerily. "You young folks bounce back. Just look at you—battling this bug these last few weeks and still determined to get up there and knock 'em dead."

Rachel understood that her recent bout with the stomach flu had gone on too long in Doc's opinion. "I'm feeling good. You need to concentrate on Paul."

But he had come anyway. Rachel glanced again at the father and son. If outward appearances were any indication, Paul had changed quite a bit since high school. Refusing to break her concentration, Rachel deliberately turned her attention to the opposite side of the hall where the judges waited.

"I want to thank y'all for the chance to sing for you again. This is a song I wrote last spring and haven't yet had a chance to perform...until tonight. I sure hope y'all like it," she said as she launched into the musical introduction. "I call it 'This Little Child,'" she added, as she began to hum along to the echoing timbre of the twelve-string guitar.

She sang the first verse with her eyes downcast, concentrating on the movement of her fingers. As she reached the first chorus she glanced at the audience and saw that she had made the right choice. She relaxed and allowed her gaze to return to Doc and Paul McCoy.

Doc was leaning forward, listening intently and smiling at her. When he saw her look his way, he gave her a subtle sign of encouragement. Doc was her biggest fan, and she was suddenly very glad he had insisted on coming.

Paul McCoy, on the other hand, was understandably less than thrilled to be there. After all, he'd just gotten off a flight from Kosovo where he'd spent the last several months treating refugees in the camps there. Like Doc, he was also a doctor, but he definitely marched to a different drummer than his father did. Paul had headed for Chicago as soon as he finished medical school. There would be no third generation of McCoy doctors in Smokey Forge as far as he was concerned. His focus had been research. The Kosovo thing had happened a few months earlier, and Rachel never had gotten it straight why he'd suddenly left a prestigious position at a top teaching hospital in Chicago to go halfway around the world.

All she knew was that he was coming back home for an indefinite amount of time to help Doc out. The rumor mill in Smokey Forge had it that Doc secretly hoped he could get Paul to stay for good. Doc was getting along in years, and ever since the death of his beloved wife, Mary, he'd been at loose ends. Publicly he claimed that Paul was just going to be around long enough to lend a hand until Doc could find a partner who would take over the practice and let him take life a little easier.

Doc continued to smile at her and nod in time to the music. Paul was slouched in his seat with his eyes closed. Rachel frowned. She didn't care how exhausted he was, nobody was going to sleep through her performance. With a renewed energy she hadn't felt in all the long, hard weeks of preparing for the talent search, she concentrated on raising the level of her performance a notch.

> And God was there
> And God could see
> This little child
> Was really me.

When she saw him open his eyes and sit up straight in his chair, she smiled and began the second verse. But her voice faltered slightly when she felt the full power of his dark eyes watching her. Paul McCoy had always been handsome in a dark, slightly intimidating sort of way. In high school, he'd had the respect of every male student and the heart of every female, but he had kept to himself—a serious student and top athlete who stayed away from school dances and social events.

The man watching her from the second row bore little physical resemblance to that boy she remembered from high school. The eyes that had stolen hearts with their burning intensity stared at her now. They did not glow with passion as they had in high school. They were dull with what she assumed was exhaustion and something more. In them she saw pain that bordered on despair and she wondered what he had seen in Kosovo that had brought him such sadness.

Certainly, her heart broke every time she saw a report on television or read a story about those poor uprooted and displaced souls. She couldn't imagine what it must be like to actually be there trying to help. It was the faces of the children that really touched her most. Those

faces had been the inspiration for the song she had chosen to perform for the finals.

> And God was there
> And God could see
> This little child
> Was really me.

Paul McCoy had watched Rachel Duke cross the
stage and noted the resemblance to her older sister
Sara—the one he'd had the crush on in high school.
He'd seen her glance at his father as they hurried to
their seats and knew that Doc had done the right thing
in coming. As she started the usual patter with the audience while she tuned her guitar, Paul had slumped
farther into his seat on the aisle.

"She's made the finals," Doc told him, having obviously picked up this bit of news from the person on
the other side of him.

"Great," Paul replied and fervently hoped that this
meant they had arrived for the grand finale of the show
and would soon be back on the road for home. At the
moment, he wanted a hot shower and a soft bed with
clean linens a lot more than he wanted to hear the Duke
kid sing. As she fingered the intricate melody of the
song, he slouched farther into his chair and closed his
eyes. At least she had chosen a ballad, he thought.

He had shut his eyes, prepared to make it through the
next hour with as little effort as possible. He was exhausted and emotionally drained from having to leave
behind unfinished work in Kosovo. Not that he could
ever have really finished his work there. Every time he
thought they were finally on the verge of a breakthrough
in the numbers of people in need of medical care, a new

flood of outcasts arrived. In spite of an end to the fighting, the new arrivals seemed more desperate than any of the masses of refugees who had come before.

Gradually, as he surrendered to the fatigue and frustration of the last several days, the music broke through the armor he had constructed for sheer emotional self-preservation. Her voice was deep and low and so rich that it seemed impossible to come from the skinny young redhead onstage. She demanded attention in a manner that was at the same time subtle and insistent. He opened his eyes and focused on the ceiling as if in doing so he might actually see the sounds floating over the hushed auditorium. He found himself straightening, sitting upright, leaning forward as his eyes locked on the waif with the huge guitar who sat alone in the center of the vast stage.

He tried dismissing the words as so much religious drivel and found he could not. He listened as if hearing a master storyteller weave a tale that was at once familiar and haunting. She sang of children lost, wandering and in need. He thought of the children in the inner-city of Chicago where he had worked before going abroad. He thought of the children that his father drove deep into the hollers (as the locals called them) and valleys of the Tennessee mountains to treat for free because they had no money to pay. For the first time since stepping onto the plane leaving Kosovo, he permitted himself to think of the children in the refugee camps. He thought of ten-year-old Samir and felt a tear escape the outer corner of one eye. He let it find its way down his cheek unchecked as he stared at the woman onstage.

There had to be a way to get the kid out of there, to get as many of them out of there as possible. The countryside was still riddled with land mines. Forget the land mines. Just drinking the water could be hazardous. He'd seen too many of the children—fatherless, motherless, alone in a place that had little time to be concerned about whether or not a kid lived or died. He'd been torn—having to choose between them and the aging widowed father who needed him, the father who had never before asked for his help. In the end, he'd come home. Sami had stood at the chain link fence watching him go. It was the only time Paul had seen the kid cry.

"You'll be okay," Paul had assured him.

"I want to come with you," Sami had pleaded, sounding for the first time like the ten-year-old kid that he was.

"Your mom needs you here." *And my dad needs me there.* It was a cheap trick, reminding a ten-year-old of responsibilities he shouldn't have. Paul felt that he, too, was abandoning the boy.

As the last note of Rachel Duke's song sailed high into the upper balcony and faded, there was utter silence for a split second before the audience roared its approval. People stood and applauded and cheered. Rachel Duke stepped forward and released the strap of her guitar. She smiled uncertainly in Doc's direction and then she collapsed onto the stage, her guitar landing next to her with a discordant thud.

In seconds the stage was alive with people crowding around her.

"Call 911," someone yelled as Paul leaped onto the stage.

"I'm a doctor," he said in a tone that parted the crowd without question. When he reached Rachel she was unconscious and so still that his heart skipped a beat. "Dad?"

"Right here, son," he heard Doc reply.

"Let's get her off this stage," Paul said. "Are you in charge here?" he asked the guy in the tuxedo.

"I can help," replied another man, who seemed far more capable. "I'm the stage manager for the theater. You can bring her backstage."

"Rachel? It's Paul McCoy. Can you open your eyes?"

*Well, of course, I can. The fact is I don't want to. How embarrassing to have my big moment and pass out cold! I poured everything I had into that performance, and now this!*

"Rachel?"

*He had a nice voice. I'd forgotten that. It was surprisingly gentle when I might have expected a more brisk professional tone. Maybe little Paulie McCoy had inherited his father's quiet, soothing bedside manner.*

"Let's get her backstage."

Rachel felt his arms go around her, lifting her. This was too much. "I can walk," she croaked, opening her eyes and finding her face too close to his for comfort.

"No doubt," he replied. "But humor me anyway." There was no hint of humor to be found in the grim, determined set of his bearded jaw. His deep-set eyes were shadowed with fatigue and seemed to dare her to test his patience.

"I'll go get my bag," she heard Doc say.

Paul carried her offstage and into a dressing room, and she could hear the emcee announcing that it was just a case of nerves and nothing to be concerned about. As Paul deposited her on a sofa and closed the door, she heard the emcee introducing the last finalist.

Paul returned to sit next to her and immediately began probing the glands under her chin and along her throat. His hands were large and warm. She felt the color rise to her cheeks.

"Bet you didn't think you'd be called into action the minute you stepped off the plane," she said in a failed attempt to lighten the moment.

"Shh," he said and frowned as he counted her pulse. "How much do you weigh?"

"Probably somewhere around one twenty," she replied.

"Probably somewhere around a hundred and five would be closer to the truth," he replied with just a hint of a reprimand. He lifted her hands and studied her unpainted nails. He frowned slightly, then patted her hands and released them. "You know, in spite of what you young women think, there *is* such a thing as being too thin."

"I…" She started to protest.

"Believe it or not, there are still people in the world who don't have enough to eat," he lectured.

Her eyes flashed in irritation. "Yes, I do know that. Perhaps you might remember that some of them live right here in the good ol' U. S. of A."

"Are you saying you don't get enough to eat?" Cynicism dripped from every word.

*So much for bedside manner,* Rachel thought and then spoke to him as if she were dealing with one of her third-grade students.

"I'm saying that you don't have a monopoly on understanding that some of us have more options than others. I'm saying that I would be as ticked off as you obviously are if I thought someone had deliberately starved herself for no good reason." She paused for a breath and delivered the clincher. "I'm *saying* that I am *not* anorexic or bulimic or anything like that, okay?"

Paul's mouth opened and shut, then opened again as he prepared his retort and then seemed to reconsider it.

"What's the verdict?" Doc asked as he entered the room and opened his medical bag.

"Not sure yet," Paul replied, stepping aside to permit his father to take over.

"What are you thinking?" Doc asked as he pulled out his stethoscope. "She's been fighting this stomach virus for the last few weeks, and we've just not been able to help her shake it."

Rachel closed her eyes again as she heard Doc relating the gory details of her illness as well as the measures they'd taken to address the symptoms. She could hear applause.

"Look, I'm fine, really. I want to know what's happening," Rachel said and tried to stand. She stumbled, and Paul caught her. She swallowed a nervous giggle as it suddenly dawned on her how many of her girlfriends in high school would have been thrilled to find themselves in the arms of Paul McCoy not once but twice in a single evening.

"Why don't I go see what they decide and you get back on that sofa, young lady?" Doc said, handing Paul the stethoscope. "You're in good hands here."

Before Rachel could stop him, Doc was gone. She faced Paul again. They traded wary glances. "How about a truce? We'll chalk your bad mood up to a long plane ride and mine up to nerves and embarrassment at falling flat on my face in front of a panel of judges I really wanted to impress."

"It was the music they were to judge, not you," he replied with maddening logic as he donned the stethoscope and prepared to use it. "Take a deep breath." He listened and moved the stethoscope. "Again."

She did as she was told. "In the first place, they may have come to judge the music, but since the music comes from me—this mouth, these fingers..." She saw that he was frowning again. "You know, you're making far too big a deal of this," she protested.

He ignored her protest and continued to listen. "Okay, regular breaths now."

"I've had a little bug, and you're right to a point. I mean, I'll admit that I probably could have eaten more nutritious meals, but..."

"Again, deep breaths and this time, try not to talk," he said quietly as he moved the cold metal just inside her blouse.

She studied the man before her and tried to relate this person to the boy she'd known. He'd been in her sister Sara's class, four years ahead of Rachel. He had always been very serious, a kid determined to come to his own conclusions rather than simply accept the rules of others. His attitude quickly earned him the label of rebel in the small, conservative community. The adults tolerated him because of their respect for his parents. The kids idolized him.

Paul never seemed to notice one way or another. The opinions of others clearly did not interest him. She tried to recall a single time Paul had permitted his carefully cultivated facade of coolness to slip. Then she did remember a time, and it made her smile. It was the day he had asked Sara to the prom. Rachel had been with Sara, and Paul had stammered and blushed so badly that he'd barely been able to get the words out. She decided to hold on to that image of him as a weapon in combating his efforts to intimidate her now.

"That was quite a performance out there," Paul said as he sat back and hung the stethoscope around his neck while he reached for a small penlight from his father's bag. "Follow the light without moving your head," he instructed as he moved the light back and forth, up and down.

"Thank you, I think. I mean that's the kind of thing a person could take either way. Sort of like what my mom used to call a left-handed compliment."

"Possibly." He put the light away and considered her for a long moment. "I have friends in Chicago who are performers. It takes a tremendous amount of energy to stay in top form. They all work hard at keeping themselves in excellent shape—diet, exercise…"

She sighed heavily. "Look, you keep hinting that I have an eating disorder. I don't," she assured him. "I eat like a horse, and bluntly put, I keep it all down. I've had this little virus lately. Other than that…" She could see that he was definitely not used to being talked to in this way.

He repeated the gentle probing of the underside of her jaw near her ears with his fingertips. "Any soreness or tenderness there?" he asked.

Warmed by the sensation of his gentle touch, Rachel shook her head in response. She knew he was not listening to her protests.

"Good." He found pen and paper on the dressing table and made a couple of notes. "Tell me about this virus."

"Nothin' but a good ol' fashioned stomach flu," she replied. "You know, throwing up, stomach cramps— all the usual attractive symptoms."

"How long did it last?"

"Doc told you—" she began, but he interrupted.

"Yes, he did. Now I'm asking you."

"It comes and goes."

He glanced up, and there was the slightest flicker of surprise in his expression. "For how long?"

"I guess it first came on about four weeks ago."

"And the most recent episode—before tonight, that is."

She laughed. "Tonight had nothing to do with the flu, Paul."

"Let me be the judge of that. Have you had previous incidents of dizziness or fainting associated with this?"

"Of course not. Maybe a little light-headedness from time to time—a couple of times, but this is the first time I've ever fainted in my life. It's not something I plan on repeating any time soon, I assure you."

He attached a blood-pressure cuff to her arm and began pumping it. "That's a little high," he said, more to himself, it seemed, than to her.

"I get a little nervous seeing doctors," she said. "Look…"

He motioned for her to be quiet as he counted her pulse again.

"So, you're *that* Duke," he said as he let go of her wrist and replaced the blood-pressure cuff in Doc's bag. "Now I remember. Dad always had some problems with you. I think I remember that there were a couple of times when you made it pretty clear that you didn't care a whole lot for doctors. That was you, wasn't it?" He remembered the freckle-faced kid she had been, with a temper to match her red hair. "As I recall, you actually bit him once for giving you a shot."

She stared at him. "Let me guess. You were absent the day they taught bedside manner, right?"

"The man had to wear a bandage for a week."

She blushed. "I apologized for that. Mama made me write a note and hand it to Doc personally."

"Well, I promise not to give you any shots. On the other hand, I would like to get you home as soon as possible and run some tests. Maybe draw a little blood. I mean, if you're telling me you aren't anorexic, I'd like to find out a little more about this virus." He began packing up his father's equipment as if her agreement were a foregone conclusion.

"I might need to stay here," she replied. "If I win," she added shyly.

"I wouldn't advise that."

"If I win the competition, I have a contract to perform," she explained as if talking to a not-so-bright child.

"Unless you get some rest and proper food, you're going to end up in the hospital," he replied as he snapped the bag shut.

Rachel decided she would take the matter up with Doc. After all, Paul was not her doctor. She relaxed on the couch and waited for Doc's return.

"Do you also sing country rock?" Paul asked. He had sat down in a chair across from her and stretched out his long legs. She understood that he, too, was deliberately closing the subject of her health, at least for the moment. "It seems to be all the rage these days."

"Strictly gospel," she replied automatically as she continued to consider her options should she win the contest.

He raised one eyebrow in surprise. "Really? Nothing but gospel?"

"Why does that surprise you?"

"I guess I just assumed that someone young like you with all that ambition would perform in the venue most likely to give you national exposure. Gospel is not exactly what wins the top Grammy awards."

She flinched defensively. "Well, it's what I do and there's always a first time."

"Sorry. I don't mean to offend you. Even though I'm hardly the model churchgoing type, I happen to enjoy gospel singing very much."

"For the music rather than the message, I assume?" she asked.

He shrugged. "It's not easy for a Smokey Forge boy to admit that he's strayed from the faith." He could not imagine why he would confide such a thing to her.

"That's too bad—I mean that you've strayed," she said, studying him long enough for him to feel slightly uncomfortable. "Admitting it is the first step toward getting back."

"Perhaps for some," he muttered as he stood and paced the small room. Instinctively, she knew that the simple words covered some deeper unspoken message.

She nodded. "It's definitely not terminal. People drop out all the time, but sooner or later, they find their way back. You will, too. God will see to that."

Paul pinned her with his dark eyes. "I know it's impossible for others to understand, but perhaps if you could have seen some of the pain and suffering I've witnessed…" He shook his head and turned away.

"So, then why did you come back home? Why leave Kosovo?" she asked when the silence between them had gone on too long.

"Dad needs some help until he can find someone to take over the clinic after he retires, and… Who knows why any of us make the choices we do?" A slight lifting of his shoulders was the end of his response as Doc opened the door and looked from her to his son and back again.

"What's the verdict?"

"I don't want to jump to conclusions, but there are a number of things that are coming together here." Paul moved closer to his father and spoke in low tones as if she were sleeping or had left the room. "Loss of weight, fatigue, an elevated heart rate and higher than normal blood pressure. This virus that she's been fighting. Is there something going around town?"

Doc shook his head. "A few cases of food poisoning about a month ago."

"I want to run some lab work, but at the very least when an otherwise healthy young woman has dizzy spells, we're dealing with something that shouldn't be ignored."

"Rachel, you never mentioned these dizzy spells," Doc said sternly.

"You're both overreacting." Rachel stood and this time she didn't need anyone to steady her. "It's nerves and burning the candle at both ends and forgetting to eat. All easily fixed. What happened out there, Doc?"

Paul read his father's face and knew she hadn't won.

"Close second, honey," he said softly and handed her the envelope with the cash prize he had collected for her.

"I see," she said softly as she fingered the envelope.

Paul watched her take a moment to digest the news. Then she turned and looked at them both with a dazzling smile. "Well, can a girl hitch a ride home with you two doctors? I should get back so I can teach tomorrow, and Paulie here wants to siphon off some blood for his tests."

Paul couldn't have been more surprised at her reaction to the news. He might have expected tears and gnashing of teeth, not having to hurriedly gather his jacket to follow her and his father down the hall.

On her way out, Rachel took time to congratulate the winner and thank each judge. She hugged the stage manager, who held her close and said something that made her laugh. There wasn't a trace of self-pity in her, Paul thought as he observed all of this. Rachel Duke was pretty poised for a kid straight out of the hills of Tennessee who had just performed on the biggest country music stage in the world. She was not at all what he might have expected.

# Chapter Two

"Yo, Dr. Paulie, how 'bout leaving some in the tank?" Rachel protested with a grin as Paul prepared to fill a second vial with blood.

It had been a busy week since they'd all returned from that night in Nashville, and she had finally come to the office to permit him to draw blood for the battery of tests he had ordered.

"Just one more," he replied. Rachel had always been the cute one in the Duke family. Her sister Sara was more serious, and Maggie, the eldest, cast into the role of mother for her siblings when their parents died, had taken to her part as earth mother with relish. When she was a child, Rachel's antics had been in keeping with her life as a much-loved child. As an adult, he would have expected the harder knocks of life to dampen some of her enthusiasm. Apparently, they hadn't, or else she had lived a sheltered and charmed life.

"You're not going to find anything, you know," she assured him. "I'm feeling better already. It was just nerves and the remnants of that flu."

She might be cute, but she was also opinionated. It always came out in an upbeat way, as if she had some secret source for inside information. "The flu does not commonly last four weeks or more," he replied, stating a fact. "Nor does it generally appear, go away and then appear again. At the very least you are borderline malnourished and dangerously exhausted." He didn't add that she had also just had what he assumed was a major disappointment in losing first place in the talent search, and such things took their own toll.

She put on a mock frown. "Gee, Dr. McCoy, the patient feels fine, and she's having no symptoms. Here's a radical thought—maybe she's not sick anymore? Maybe she just needs a week or so and a couple of hot fudge sundaes to get back on her feet?"

"Don't you ever have a bad day?" he asked, studying her closely for any sign that she was putting on some kind of act to cover more serious symptoms.

Rachel shrugged and grinned. "Life's pretty amazing."

He made no reply to that as he released the elastic tourniquet on her arm and pulled out the syringe.

"I'm a quick healer, Paul. Always have been," she assured him, refusing a bandage. "Looks like you could have used one earlier yourself."

She pointed to the place on his chin where he had nicked himself shaving that morning. Her finger came just short of touching him, and he wondered why that disappointed him. "I'm a little out of practice."

"How come you took off the beard?"

He shrugged. "I just let it grow out in Kosovo. Not a lot of time for shaving over there." He tried to make light of it. Instead he found it hard to disguise the painful memories that came with any thought of his experience there, much less the guilt he couldn't shake at having left his work unfinished. He had shaved because every time he looked in the mirror, he found himself back there. He could hardly expect Rachel Duke to understand that.

"So, was it as bad as all the reports say?" For the first time all morning, her expression was serious and filled with concern. Her voice was low and soft as if she wanted to know but didn't want to intrude.

Paul stifled an urge to give a sarcastic laugh. "What reports? Kosovo is pretty much forgotten ever since the fighting stopped. The media have lost interest."

"I'm sorry. It's understandable that you might not be ready to talk about it. It must have been pretty awful." She paused and then put her hand on his. "You know, sometimes it really is good to talk these things out. I mean, stuffing all those memories and feelings inside…" She saw something in his expression that stopped her from finishing her thought. "On the other hand," she said, deliberately changing her tone as well as the topic, "I know that Doc is really glad you decided to come home for a while before heading back to Chicago."

"I'm not sure I'm going back to Chicago," Paul said and wished he hadn't. He wasn't ready to share his plans and he didn't want to raise false hopes for his father. What was it about her that had him blurting out these things? "That is, it could take some time to get somebody in here to help Dad. Besides I could use some time to take stock." There, he'd done it again.

Rachel laughed. "Some things never change, Paul McCoy. You always were one to go off somewhere alone to lick your wounds or plan your next move. It was a huge part of your charm when you were sixteen.

We'll have to see how it plays now that you're twice that.''

She stood and headed for the door. As she passed him, she playfully ruffled his hair. ''Welcome home, Dr. McCoy.''

A couple of days later he found himself warmed by the memory as he squinted at the slide under his microscope and then sat back and thought about the kid he had known. Rachel had been all arms and legs as a youngster and shown none of the promise of beauty that she had grown into as an adult. She'd always been tagging along with her older sisters, even on that awful day when he'd finally worked up the nerve to invite Sara Duke to the prom.

He realized now that it was Rachel's face rather than Sara's he recalled most clearly from that day. He recalled her look of fascination at his stumbling, bumbling attempt to impress Sara Duke with his coolness. In that moment he had dropped his carefully constructed facade of the serious, studious loner and revealed to the world his desperate hope that Sara would say yes. Rachel had seen his vulnerability that day, and she couldn't have been more than fourteen. Earlier this week, he had once again exposed his vulnerability to her, and she'd picked up on it just as quickly as before. The idea that Rachel Duke could see right through him was a little unsettling.

He glanced out the window and back to the slide he'd been holding. It was a glorious autumn day, and for reasons he couldn't quite grasp, he suddenly felt like enjoying it. No doubt, Rachel would assure him that this was a positive result of all those dreary months in Kosovo. Still, taking a break for a walk over to the café for a sandwich seemed perfectly in order.

"Ruby," he said to the receptionist who had worked with his father for over twenty years, "tell Dad I took an early lunch."

Rachel sat alone on a park bench in the middle of the town square. She glanced through the flaming orange leaves of the maple and grinned. "Well, God, I guess I'm here at the burning bush. You know, I thought it would be easier to accept not winning the other night, but the truth is I really wanted that contract. I'm trying hard to understand why You think I ought to be happy just staying here in Smokey Forge, teaching the kids and playing the local revival circuit, but..."

She shook off her objections. "Sorry," she said meekly. "It's just I'm trying to understand what it is I'm supposed to do. I mean, You gave me this talent, and surely..."

She took a deep breath. She knew better than to debate with God. "The thing is, I could use a little guidance here if You're not too busy with other things right now." She closed her eyes for a minute, then opened them and saw Paul McCoy walking across the square toward her.

"This is Your answer?" she whispered, glancing heavenward for assurance. "This is Your sign? Paul McCoy?" She watched Paul coming closer and took a deep breath. "Well, okay, but I don't get it. I don't get it at all."

"Rachel?" Paul covered the distance between them and looked around. "Who are you talking to?"

"God," she replied without hesitation, and taking in his look of abject disbelief, she added, "We chat from time to time. I think He sent you to Nashville the other night just in the nick of time to rescue me, and now, at this particular moment, so I guess we need to talk—at least until I can figure out your part in all of this.'' She patted the bench beside her to indicate that he should sit down.

''I see.''

She understood that he didn't see at all and that he was amused by the situation. She was used to that, although it made her sad that so many people did not have the kind of open loving relationship with God that she had known throughout her life.

''So what does God want from me?'' he asked.

''A great deal, judging by the fact that He entrusted His children in Kosovo to your care, not to mention all those poor people in Chicago and now everyone here in Smokey Forge.''

''You're not making a lot of sense,'' he said. She noticed that he had begun to frown the moment she mentioned Kosovo.

''Well, it's just that you were supposed to be in Kosovo or Chicago. I was hoping to be in Nashville, and here we are. Doc tells me I have the flu, but you right away see that it might be something else. Makes me reconsider some of my symptoms.''

''You're still not feeling well,'' he finished quietly, and studied her.

''I'm feeling fine, but the way you reacted the other night and now drawing these blood samples and all, I'm guessing you think this is more than just the garden-variety stomach flu. I'm also guessing you might have seen something similar in Kosovo?''

She was pretty perceptive for someone untrained in medical science. ''I'd just like to know more about what led up to your passing out the other night.''

Rachel nodded. ''I can't really say. I mean, I've always been so healthy,'' she said softly. ''I was just so sure that it was just getting over this bug and the excitement of the performance and all, but it's beginning to make sense that it might be something more. I mean, for me to have so little energy is unheard of—ask anyone in town.''

''I'm afraid prior good health plays no favorites in people becoming ill, Rachel, although that is certainly in your favor when it comes to getting well. Tell me what's happening.''

She had his complete attention now, and it was disconcerting. ''It's weird. Most of the time, I'm feeling great and then out of the blue...I just feel...I don't know...punky.''

He blinked. ''Punky?''

''Yeah, not really sick but less than my best. I still don't seem to have much energy. I mean I eat like a horse—honestly.'' She glanced at her flat stomach.

''Punky.'' He repeated the word to himself.

''It's a family thing,'' Rachel explained. ''That's how Mom helped us describe our symptoms when we were kids.''

''I'm going to need a little more to go on than that,'' he said, but his voice was more gentle than normal.

''What about the blood you took the other day?''

''Inconclusive,'' he replied, and frowned again. She could see that Paul McCoy still liked to have clear-cut answers to problems.

''But what do you think?'' she asked after a moment.

''If you're not anorexic—which, believe me, I am not convinced you're not—is there any chance you could have come in contact with some contaminated water?''

To his surprise, she laughed. ''Me? Heavens, no. Ask anybody in town, and they'll tell you I am religious about drinking the bottled stuff exclusively. Abigail down at the market orders a case of it every week just for me. It's my one vice.''

"It's not unheard of for bottled water to become contaminated. Can I get a sample to check?''

"Well, sure, but how could that possibly relate to what you saw in Kosovo?''

"While I was there, we saw a number of cases of this certain type of parasite. You have a lot of the same symptoms. I contacted a friend of mine in Chicago who has been researching this parasite. He's quite interested in the idea that it might have shown up here as well as overseas.''

"Doc treated a few other people around the same time that I got sick, but they had symptoms that were more like food poisoning.''

Paul nodded. "The symptoms are pretty similar in milder cases. I take it those people recovered quickly?''

She nodded. "Why would that be? I mean why would theirs go away while mine came and went for weeks, and why didn't anybody else get it—if it's in the water, then…''

"It's probably not the water you drink. It may not even be water that's local to here, but there has to be some common element.'' He was talking more to himself than to her.

"Okay, so what do we need to do?'' she prodded.

"Let's start by testing the water. In the meantime I'd like to prescribe some antibiotics for you, just as a precaution.''

Rachel reached into the canvas bag that served as her purse. She handed him a half-filled bottle of water. "Is this enough to test?''

Paul nodded and took the water. "I'll call in a prescription to the pharmacy as soon as I get back to the office.''

"If you don't mind, Paul, I'd like to keep this between us, at least until you know more. Maggie's already in serious mother mode ever since I first got sick." She blushed and gave a nervous little laugh.

"Having somebody to watch over you doesn't sound like such a bad idea.''

"I know it's silly but I've worked pretty hard to break the apron strings, so to speak. My sisters have finally started to view me as a grown-up. If Maggie gets the idea that this is anything serious…" Rachel rolled her eyes.

"I really don't think you need to be overly concerned, Rachel, and by the way, believe it or not, I understand about your need to break away," Paul said, and made a sound that bordered on a chuckle. "How do you think it was for me, being the only son and grandson of the doctors who have treated everybody in town for decades?"

"Why, Dr. McCoy, are you suggesting that we're two of a kind? Imagine that," she replied and stood to gather her things. "Well, I've got classes in an hour. I'll stop by the pharmacy after school.''

"Do you have to get back right away?" he asked. "Have you had lunch?''

"Paul, I do eat. You don't have to feed me," she assured him, the mega-watt smile firmly in place.

"I'm not asking in my professional capacity," he protested. "Honestly. I haven't eaten and if you haven't, then why not eat together? You can catch me up on all the gossip.''

She looked at him with suspicion. "Since when do you have any interest in gossip?''

"Try me. Maybe I've changed."

Rachel laughed. "Oh, I get it. I bet you just want to get the scoop on Sara—she's not married, you know."

"Really?"

They walked across the square together.

"She's still gorgeous."

"No doubt."

"You might have a shot," she added. "If you play your cards right."

"Hmm."

She punched him hard in the arm. "If we're going to do lunch, Paul McCoy, you're going to have to stop talking in doctorspeak."

"But I am a doctor. That's the way we talk."

"You're also a red-blooded American male who once had a serious case of the hots for my sister. I don't believe for one minute that you aren't curious about what's happened to Sara since you ran off to medical school."

"And, as I recall, you were always this sassy kid who drove your sisters crazy."

"A sassy kid who was usually right," she retorted with a grin as they entered the café together.

After lunch Rachel taught her afternoon music classes at the school and stayed late to give some private lessons. She thought about the possibility that Paul and Sara might actually strike up a romance and liked the idea very much. Sara was far too serious and enmeshed in her work. She could use a little love in her life—a little happiness.

Rachel was humming as she climbed the hill to the house where she had grown up and now lived with her two older sisters and younger twin brothers when they weren't off at college. Nothing would make her happier than for each of her two sisters to find true love. Then maybe they would stop worrying about her and she could get on with her life—and her dream of spreading God's joy through her music. She wondered what Paul McCoy's dream was. She wondered if he even thought in terms of fulfilling a dream. As close as she and her sisters had been to Paul's parents, she realized that he had usually been absent when the two families got together. He'd always had some excuse—basketball practice or a paper that was due. Once he'd left Smokey Forge for college and medical school, he hadn't come home very often, and then his visits had been short. Paul McCoy was an unknown entity in the unique dynamics of their two families. She doubted that anything would change now that he was back in town.

Maggie was sitting on the porch swing grading papers. Rachel squared her shoulders, put on her brightest smile and willed herself to walk with a lightness she didn't feel. The long afternoon of teaching and the short walk from the school had sapped her energy. One thing she had to agree with—she needed to rebuild her strength.

"Hi," she called out to Maggie as she climbed the porch stairs. "What's new?"

"Not much. Sometimes I feel as if I've graded these same papers a hundred times before," Maggie replied with a laugh. "You look a little done in."

"I'm just a little tired."

"Honey, you've been *a little tired* for over six weeks now. What did Paul say about those blood tests?"

Rachel considered her options. She had never been able to outright lie to Maggie, so her best bet was to stick as close to the truth as possible. "He's going to give me some medicine—antibiotics—just as a precaution."

Maggie studied her, looking for any sign of deception. "Maybe Doc should have another look at you."

"Doc isn't going to find anything different. Honestly, Maggie, Paul does have an actual degree and everything."

"Well, I just think that Doc knows your history. You've lived your entire life at ninety miles an hour and you seem intent on doing that until the day you drop. At the rate you're going that'll be sooner rather than later."

Rachel grinned. "Maggie, it's going to be okay. You'll see," she assured her big sister. "I'm going to rehearse awhile," she called as she entered the house, allowing the screen door to bang shut behind her. "I've got to get ready for the revival over at Codger's Cave this weekend."

"You could skip that," Maggie said. "You could actually take a few days to just sit on the porch here and strum your guitar or read a book."

"Can't let folks down if you're able to be there," Rachel replied. "You're the one who taught us all that."

"Me and my big mouth," Maggie grumbled to herself. She could hear Rachel gathering her music and guitar and heading out the back. "Be home for supper," she called as the phone rang. She waited for the second ring to see if Rachel might come back to answer, but she was already halfway across the yard, headed for the path to the mill. With a resigned sigh, Maggie pushed herself off the swing and went inside to answer the phone.

"Maggie? Hi, it's Paul McCoy."

"Well, Paulie, how nice to have you back home. I hear you saw my baby sister earlier today. Want to tell me why she's so thin and tired?"

"Now, Maggie, you know as well as I do I can't discuss that with you," he said, his tone strictly business.

Maggie laughed. "I thought it was worth a shot."

"Is she there?"

"No, not right now. You just missed her. Can I give her a message?"

"No, nothing important. I'll catch up with her later."

"You come on by any time—how about supper tonight? Sara will be here. The twins are off at college, but Mattie came in for a few days. He's got himself a girlfriend, and it's beginning to look pretty serious. Seems impossible, but there you have it. She's coming to meet us all tonight so you might as well be there, too. Matt will be as nervous as a cat in a room full of rocking chairs. Maybe having another male here will help. So, you'd be more than welcome."

"I'll see how things are going at the clinic," Paul told her, not wanting to commit to the evening.

"Don't stand on ceremony," Maggie replied. "Just show up. There's always plenty of food. We sit down around six."

He promised again to think about it and hung up. He tried to figure out why on earth he had not turned down the invitation to supper. It had certainly never been difficult before. In fact, it had almost been automatic. It surprised him to realize that not only was he considering the invitation, he was looking forward to it.

"Ridiculous," he muttered as he gathered the notes he'd made on Rachel's bottled water. Clearly, he had considered the idea because that would be an obvious way to see Rachel and tell her the water was clean. He certainly didn't need to go to supper to accomplish that.

"Ruby, tell Dad I've gone for the day," he said as he hung up his lab coat and headed for the door. "I'm going to check on a patient."

He left the clinic that occupied a storefront office on Main Street and drove through town. He had no idea where he was headed, but he hadn't wanted to raise further questions by asking Maggie how to find Rachel. Her comment about trying to break out from under the shadow of her sisters' achievements had struck a chord with him. How well he remembered the pressure he'd put on himself to live up to the spotless reputations of his father and grandfather. Rachel deserved a chance to make her own decisions and follow her own dreams.

As he drove through town, he saw a number of people he'd grown up with. They waved or called out to him, and he waved back. He realized that it was certainly not as difficult as he might have thought to come here. Actually, it was even pleasant to feel part of a community that went beyond hospital walls, to be in a place that was so completely normal and safe after what he had witnessed in Kosovo.

On the outskirts of the small village was the charter elementary school that the parents of the Dukes had started before they died. Maggie and Sara had taken over after they finished college. Knowing that Rachel taught music at the school, he wondered if she might possibly be there even though classes were out for the day. A car was in the lot so he pulled in and headed for the entrance.

"Paul McCoy, look at you."

Sara Duke was every bit as beautiful as Paul remembered, but he felt nothing of the spark he had always wrestled with upon seeing her in high school. "Did you dump me for some other guy yet?" he said as he walked up the path to the school.

"Maybe. I could hardly be expected to stand around waiting for you to decide to come home where you belong," she replied. Then she hugged him. "You look great. How's Doc?"

"Firmly in charge of things, but glad to have me home, especially now that Mom's gone. I think it got pretty lonesome for him rattling around in that big ol' house."

Sara nodded. "He was so excited when you agreed to come back until he could find someone to join the practice. That was a really hard thing for him to do, you know. Ask for your help. He knew how important your work was to you and he felt guilty about taking you away from people who needed you more than he thought he did. He talks about you constantly—a very proud papa."

"That's embarrassing," Paul said with a grin and glanced around, hoping to catch a glimpse of Rachel.

"Well, now, obviously you didn't just stop by to chat. How can I help?"

"I thought maybe Rachel might be here."

"Rachel? No, I haven't seen her. Maggie called and said you'd given her a prescription for some antibiotics. She's going to be okay then?"

Paul nodded. "I just forgot to tell her one thing— nothing major. I was driving by and saw your car. I thought she might be here."

Sara smiled with relief. "That's really sweet of you, Paul. I have no idea where she is. Did you check up at the house?"

"Maggie said she left a little while ago."

"Then check the old mill. She goes there sometimes to play her guitar and write her music. She's probably rehearsing for the revival she's playing this weekend over at Codger's Cove."

Paul turned to go. "Thanks, I'll do that."

"Hey, we're all getting together for supper at the house tonight. Why don't you come?"

"Maggie already asked me," Paul replied and waved as he hurried to his car.

When Paul reached the mill, he saw Rachel sitting by the stream. She was playing her guitar, and he thought he had never seen anyone who looked more at peace with the world than she did. He envied her that. It was one of the things he had come back to Smokey Forge to find.

"Did you write that?" he asked when the last chord had died away.

She jumped at the sound of his voice but immediately composed herself. "It's just something I'm working on."

He sat on the bank of the creek a little away from her. "I got the preliminary results from the water test. They were negative."

"That was fast."

He shrugged. "They're not as conclusive as the results I'll get back from the state lab, but I've set up a little lab in the clinic, and the initial results are in."

She glanced at him then studied the tumbling creek. "So, if it is the parasite, it's not from the water."

"At least not from that water."

"It's the only water I drink," she reminded him.

"Yeah. I was wondering about that. It raises some interesting questions."

"Such as?"

"Well, if you only drink bottled water and this is a waterborne parasite, and it wasn't in the water you drink..."

"Of course, it could have been in a bottle I drank several weeks ago, couldn't it?"

He admired the way her mind worked. "Or you might have come in contact with the parasite in some other manner. I understand that you're performing at a revival this weekend?"

"Codger's Cove, but I don't see what..."

"Do you eat or drink at these things?"

"Sometimes."

"Just to be on the safe side, take your own food and water with you this time, okay?"

There didn't seem to be anything left to say, and yet he made no move to leave.

"I really liked that melody you were playing when I came. Could I hear it again?"

She nodded and nervously strummed the guitar. She was used to performing in front of large crowds of people as well as friends and family members, but the thought of playing in front of Paul suddenly made her shy. She fingered the tune for several bars.

"It goes on like that," she said.

"I was surprised when Dad told me that not winning first place meant that, at least for now, you were going to give up trying to make it as an entertainer," he said.

"I never aspired to be an entertainer in the way I think you mean it," she replied.

"You tried out for a performing contract at the Grand Ole Opry," he reminded her.

"I remember that," she said with a grin. "I was there."

It took him a few seconds to realize that she was gently teasing him.

"Well, yeah, but isn't that why you did it? I mean, don't you want to be a big-time star some day?"

"Not really. I thought that if I won the talent search it would be a sign that God wanted me to take that route in spreading His message through my music." She shrugged. "He obviously has some other plan in mind, and now I just need to wait and see what that might be."

He considered this for a minute. "You won second place," he reminded her.

"And maybe one day that will lead to something, but for now, I am a teacher of music and I write songs. It's a very good life." She punctuated her summation with a strum on the guitar. "Why did you decide to be a doctor?"

"We're not talking about me," he reminded her.

"Maybe we should," she replied and met his gaze.

# *Chapter Three*

He hesitated. Her directness was surprising and unsettling.

"Come on," she coached, "I'll help get you started. Back in Chicago you…" She made a pulling motion with her hands as if towing a boat to shore. "Come on. There must have been some reason you dropped everything and took off for Kosovo for three months."

"Back in Chicago I was spinning my wheels," he said matter-of-factly, and was prepared to leave it at that. But she remained silent, watching him, waiting for more. "The hospital was mired in bureaucracy, and making any kind of real difference was next to impossible." He stopped and bowed his head to avoid her gaze.

"So you left," she said quietly.

He glanced away. "Do you play a lot of these regional revivals?" he asked, signaling an end to any further personal conversation.

"But why Kosovo?" she persisted, ignoring his attempt to change subjects.

He frowned. "I couldn't tell you. The opportunity came up. It was a spur-of-the-moment decision, and once I was there..." He was obviously prepared to leave it at that as he strolled closer to the rushing stream.

"I think God sent you there, just like He's brought you home now."

Paul turned and faced her. "I don't believe that, Rachel," he said sternly. For the first time her determination to draw him out seemed shaken. "Look," he continued, "I know that stuff helps a lot of people—clearly, it's meaningful to you, but..."

"It's not about whether it helps or not," she argued stubbornly. "It's just the way it is. It's the way the world works."

He stared at her for a long moment, and in his eyes she saw such sadness that it was like watching a person in great pain.

"No, Rachel. Believe me, I know how easy it is to buy into that when you've lived your whole life in these mountains, but it's not the way the world works. The world can be horrific and cruel. It's filled with people whose only concern is for themselves and the power they can wield. It's filled with nations who have hated each other for so long that they can't even remember where it all started."

"If everyone believed that, nothing would ever get accomplished. People would just throw up their hands," she said with absolute certainty and no rancor. "And by the way, it's very unattractive, you know—that big-city snobbery that says you can't know the world until you've walked the mean streets."

"I am not a snob," he protested, but she could see that she had succeeded in breaking his somber mood.

"Yes, you are, and in some ways you always were, Paul McCoy. Fortunately you were gorgeous enough to get away with it."

"So, you think I'm gorgeous?" he asked, his face a mask of seriousness. Still, she did not miss the hint of mischief in his deep-set eyes.

"I used the past tense," she reminded him. "You *were* gorgeous for a high school senior and in comparison to the rest of the local talent in those days."

He actually laughed, and she realized it was the first time she'd really heard him laugh out loud. She liked the sound of it.

"Why, Dr. McCoy, beneath that gloomy exterior, could there actually be a sense of humor?"

"Let's get back to your condition," he said. "Just because there was no contamination in the bottled water doesn't mean we stop looking for the cause. With your permission I'd like to track your case. It would be a major step forward for my friend's research if this turned out to be the same parasite he's been tracking in Kosovo."

"You want me to be a lab rat for your friend's research?"

"Yeah. Something like that. Contributing to Dan's research project could give me a chance to help the people I left in Kosovo. Will you do it?" His eyes reflected some of the fire she remembered from the old days.

She stared at him, looking for any sign that he was joking. What she saw was a man who was totally serious. "This is going to be like looking for a needle in a haystack. Why not just accept that I had it and move on? Why does it matter how I got sick if we know what it is and can treat it if it comes back again?"

"If there were others in town showing the same symptoms, even if their cases were milder than yours, I'd like to include them in our effort to gather data. Anything that we can learn about your case as well as the others would be helpful."

"Including those children you saw with the same symptoms in Kosovo?"

He nodded. "Well, sure. Frankly, it would be nice to feel like I'm still helping even though I'm over here now."

"Do you regret so much that you left them?"

"A little torn would be closer to the truth. I'm not saying I didn't make the right decision coming home to help Dad, but…"

"But your work there wasn't finished," she added.

"No. On the other hand, if we can discover the source of the parasite here, Rachel, then I can have the best of both worlds—doing what I need to do to help Dad and helping my colleagues continue to fight at least one condition in Kosovo."

She was flattered that he obviously had no reservations about trusting her. Paul had always been extremely cautious about involving others in his projects.

"Well, listen to this, God," she said to the blue skies above in a perfectly normal conversational tone. "I can help Paul help those kids over there and not even leave town. Of course, that's why You brought him back here in the first place, right? That and the fact that there are people here who need him, too." She nodded knowingly as if she could both see and hear the unseen third party, then she turned to Paul.

"Works for me," she said with a smile. "Number-one lab rat at your service, Doc. How do we begin?"

"Maybe supper would be a good idea. You seem to

be having some serious hallucinations. Maggie and Sara have both invited me, and if we leave now we can just make that six o'clock sit-down time Maggie gave me."

"Ah, you've seen Sara."

"Yeah, I stopped by the school."

"She practically lives at the school," Rachel said in a tone that made it clear that she thought her sister could find better uses for her time.

"Well, she always was dedicated to whatever project she took on."

"Is that why you liked her in high school?"

"Hey, what is this—the third degree? I thought we were going to eat." He loaded her guitar into the back seat of his car, then held open the passenger door for her.

There were already several cars in the driveway when they arrived, so they had to park on the road and walk the rest of the way.

"They're all on the porch," Rachel said, and Paul heard a hint of nervousness in her tone. "I mean they'll wonder how we came to be together."

"Yep. Folks in town have already been speculating about the two of us. I'm pretty sure our having lunch earlier today was major news. Ruby knew it by the time I got back to the office. Now supper at your sister's?" He gave a shocked intake of breath that made Rachel laugh. "What *is* going on here?"

"You know, actually…" An idea was beginning to take shape. Maybe if Sara thought Paul was attracted to her little sister, she would pay more attention. "What do you say we give them something to really talk about?" she suggested with a mischievous grin. She took his hand as she led the way to the porch. "Come

on, Paul, live a little," she chided when she saw him
hesitate. "Just follow my lead. It'll be fun."

"I'm not good at *fun*," he muttered.

Rachel chose to ignore that last statement. "Hey, everybody, look who I found down by the old millstream," she called gaily as they climbed the warped
steps of the front porch.

Paul sensed that everyone had already been discussing the two of them as he and Rachel had come up the
hill from the car. He knew that Rachel was trying to
play on that curiosity. What on earth was he doing here,
and how had this pint-size dynamo coaxed him into
being part of her scheme? He let go of Rachel's hand
and turned to Maggie. "Am I still invited for supper?"

"That depends," Maggie said with a stern frown.

"On what?"

"On whether or not you've been keeping something
from me, young man."

"You mean this?" Rachel asked, grabbing his hand
again and holding it aloft as if he'd just been proclaimed
the winner of a prizefight.

"It's all over town that the two of you had lunch
together—now you show up a few hours later holding
hands?" Maggie shook her head in mock disapproval.

Paul shrugged. "We got to talking and, well, you
know your little sister here—she's pretty hard to ignore.
Actually, we found out we have a lot in common."

"Well, I'll be," Sara murmured, but she looked
pleased. Rachel sighed. This was not going at all the
way she had planned. Sara was supposed to be cool to
the idea of a possible relationship between Rachel and
Paul. Instead, she was clearly delighted.

"Now you listen to me, Paul McCoy," Maggie continued sternly. "If you think you can come on back here

to Smokey Forge and bring your city slicker ways with you and take advantage of my baby sister, you'd best think again.''

"Oh, Maggie, lighten up before you scare the poor guy off," Matt said as he crossed the porch and offered his hand to Paul. "Welcome home, Dr. McCoy. This is my girlfriend, Lisa, and we'd both like to thank you for taking the family spotlight off of us.''

Paul nodded at the pretty young woman seated on the porch railing then turned his attention to Matt. "I think your big sister there is a little upset with me," he said in a stage whisper.

"Nah. She's just trying to embarrass you.''

Paul looked at Maggie for confirmation and was not surprised to see her burst into laughter as she hugged her brother. "I never could fool this one," she said. "He always saw right through me. Well, come on in. Soup's on. Let's eat.''

At the supper table Maggie made a big deal of arranging the seating so that Paul and Rachel were next to each other. Meanwhile Rachel worked hard to keep Paul's attention focused on Sara, asking her questions about the school, telling Paul how Sara had single-handedly gotten grants to keep the school running when funding had run low. She saw that he was impressed and she liked the fact that he and Sara seemed to talk easily. Maybe her plan would work, after all.

"I've made a special celebration pie," Maggie announced, presenting her lemon pie with its lightly browned meringue piled high on top. "This was to be a pie to celebrate Rachel winning second place at the talent show, but perhaps..." She eyed Rachel and Paul.

Rachel blushed. "That's real nice, Maggie. Thanks.''

After the table had been cleared and everyone had

pitched in to make sure the dishes were done and put away, they all sat on the porch talking and drinking coffee until nearly ten.

"I'd better go," Paul said. "Thank you, Maggie, for inviting me."

"It's good to have you home," Maggie assured him.

He turned to Rachel. "Walk me to my car?"

*No,* Rachel wanted to protest. *Ask Sara.* But Sara had already busied herself collecting the last of the coffee mugs and taking them inside. Rachel saw Sara give Maggie a nudge and indicate that she should also come inside.

"Sure." They walked across the yard, aware that Rachel's family was watching them. "Sorry about that," Rachel said.

"What?"

"I was just trying to have a little fun with Maggie and take some of the pressure off of Matt. I'm afraid that things got a little out of hand back there, and now Maggie and Sara think we're...you know...a couple."

"Yeah. Bummer."

"I'm serious, Paul. You don't know my sisters. By morning, they'll have us in a full-blown romance. They're probably peeking out the windows and wondering why you don't kiss me good-night."

He grinned and stroked her cheek. "Why, Ms. Duke, I thought you'd never ask," he said and leaned in to kiss her gently on the forehead. It was hard to say which of them was more surprised at his action.

"I...didn't mean...you..." Rachel sputtered as she felt the soft warmth of his lips on her forehead. "Just go," she whispered, taking a deliberate step away from him. She couldn't tell him she wanted to match him with Sara. That would make things just too awkward between Sara and him.

Paul got into his car. "I had a good time tonight, Rachel. I'll see you tomorrow. Get some sleep," he ordered. "I want to get started on collecting our data. The first thing I need to get is a thorough history of where you've been that you might have picked up the bug. I'll be by at seven to take you to breakfast."

"You don't need to feed me."

"I can see that. I don't know when I've seen a woman pack it away the way you do at mealtime," he teased. "If I didn't suspect you had been infected by a parasite, I'd wonder where you were putting all of that food."

"I have a very high metabolism," she said, huffing, "and I don't eat *that* much."

"No, I'd say most young women your age take thirds on Maggie's lemon pie."

"It was a sliver. Don't you have any other patients to harass?"

"Not yet. I'm new in town, remember? Be ready at seven and start thinking about where else you might have picked up this bug of yours."

"I have to be at school by eight-thirty," she called as he drove away.

He acknowledged that bit of information with a wave and kept driving. Rachel stood watching the taillights of his car until he turned the corner.

"You know, other people have important stuff to do, too," she muttered to herself as she walked back up the hill to the house. She glanced at the star-filled sky. "I could use a little help here, You know. I can handle the medical part, but getting him together with Sara is in Your hands, okay?"

\* \* \*

Over the next few weeks they fell into an uneasy pattern of working together. Her eternal optimism was disconcerting, to say the least. Paul felt the necessity to instruct her in the science of data collection, showing her that following a rational path did not always end in the answers a person hoped would be there at the end. Undaunted, she kept challenging him. Every time he asked why, she was more interested in *what if.*

Not that Rachel felt she could offer much help, but she found the whole process interesting and she couldn't keep herself from wanting to know what he might have discovered while she was busy teaching third-graders to play the recorder.

Some days she would come out of school at the end of the day and find him waiting for her. Together they would head to the library at the small private college in town. There she would take notes while he searched through the documents and articles he could find on the library's link to the Internet, while he waited for his own computer and files to be shipped from Chicago. As they drove from place to place, he would continue to ask questions and dictate notes that he would later send Dan in Chicago.

While he waited for her to finish teaching, he would lean against his car reading some article in an old medical journal he had found in his father's office.

"You should come inside sometime. Sara's office is right there," Rachel told him once, after her classes were over. She pointed to a window near the entrance. "She always has the coffeepot on."

"This is fine. Gives me a chance to catch up on my reading. Besides, I just got here a couple of minutes ago."

One particularly blustery afternoon, she noticed that his jacket was open, as usual, while she was hastily buttoning her sweater.

"I don't know why you have to be so stubborn about coming inside. Sara has other things to occupy her, and you could read in her office. She won't bite, you know."

"Rachel, I'm not afraid of your sister—anymore, that is. This isn't high school."

"Suit yourself. Go ahead and freeze," she said, grousing as the wind picked up dry leaves and swirled them around her ankles.

"I'm used to it, remember. I used to work and live in the Windy City. Are you going to be warm enough?"

"For the library? I don't know if you've noticed, but that place is usually hotter than Florida in mid-August."

"I've been thinking that maybe we'd take a different approach. I seem to recall that there are a lot of creeks and streams back in the country."

"*This* is the country," she reminded him.

"Naw, this is *town*. I mean back thar in them hil-ahs," he said in an exaggerated drawl.

"Hil-ahs?"

"Hills. Hollers. The sticks?"

He made her laugh. Serious, intense Paul McCoy was making a joke.

"What do you hope to prove?" she asked.

He held up empty glass vials. "Once we collect samples, Dan can test the water and figure out where this bug lives."

"That makes sense. Let's go."

"What? No questions? No buts? I'm shocked, Ms. Duke."

"*Now*, he finds that offbeat sense of humor," she muttered and got into the car.

They spent several afternoons climbing through the hills to remote creeks and streams and collecting samples. All the while she would remind him that she hadn't been in contact with any of the water he was testing.

More often than not, it seemed only natural to stop by the clinic, pick up Doc and head to the farm for one of Maggie's bountiful suppers. Before Paul knew what was happening, he was spending more time at the Duke house then he was at his dad's. Not only that, he looked forward to the evenings he spent there.

After supper, Rachel usually made a point of going off with friends or up to her room to rehearse, leaving Paul with Sara and the others. Sara was very good at asking questions about the research—better than Rachel was. Sara understood the science of what his friend was trying to discover and prove, and Rachel could not help noticing how Paul's eyes lit up whenever Sara asked about the project.

In addition to playing chauffeur and secretary for his research, Rachel still stopped by the clinic for regular checkups and to permit him to draw more blood.

"You've tested negative for the parasite ever since you started the antibiotics," he told her one afternoon.

"You sound a little disappointed," she teased him.

"Heavens, no," he protested, then realized she was joking. "Cute. You've gained five pounds."

"Where?" she said twisting around to check out her backside. "Well, no more of Maggie's chocolate cake for me."

"The fact that you're gaining back some weight is a good thing," he reminded her.

"Who are you all of a sudden? Martha Stewart?"

"You're singing better than ever," he commented, knowing the way to her heart was to praise her talent.

"You really think so?"

He smiled.

"Oh, you. You'd say anything to make me think you were some kind of miracle healer. You always had this enormous ego."

"And you, as I recall, were always able to charm your way out of anything you didn't want to do."

"I was a very good kid," she protested.

"Uh-huh," he replied with a skeptical lift of his eyebrows.

And that's the way things went. Before Rachel knew what had happened she was working with Paul McCoy to find answers to the mysterious parasite. She didn't fool herself into thinking there might be anything more to it on his part than work. He was a scientist. She had a condition that interested him and was a departure from the routine ailments he and Doc treated at the clinic. He was a man who searched for answers to questions that raised his professional curiosity. On top of that, it was clear that he liked her and her family and enjoyed their company. On the other hand, he was Paul McCoy, dedicated to his work, fated to do great things and destined to do them anywhere besides Smokey Forge, Tennessee. From that standpoint, they were a good match, because Rachel also dreamed of doing great things in bigger places.

For Paul, spending most of his free time with Rachel and her family started the night she decided to have some fun with her family and drew him into her mischief. As a kid Paul had played by the rules, but he was always in control. Rachel's spontaneity and constant good humor kept him off balance, and yet he looked forward to spending time with her. He enjoyed talking about his research with Sara, but he especially liked getting Rachel's unique perspective on his work. She raised illogical questions that would never occur to him.

He thought about her as he had always thought about her when they'd all been in high school. She was Sara's younger sister—the cute one, the one with the overactive imagination, and these days, the one who made him smile. She made no demands on him or his time. In fact, he sometimes worried that he was imposing too much on her time. They each had a dream to do something bigger with their talent, and he reminded himself that it was important that he not keep her from focusing on her dream while he pursued his own.

He was aware that she was trying to play the matchmaker between Sara and him. He suspected Sara was aware of it, as well, and amused by the antics of her younger sister. The truth was he liked Sara, but any romantic feelings he might have felt in the past simply weren't there. Still, he kind of enjoyed watching Rachel try her hand at matchmaking.

"So, let's talk about this thing you and Sara used to have for each other," she said casually one afternoon after she had dropped off some articles she had copied for him on the school's copy machine.

"If you're referring to that disastrous crush I had on your sister when we were juniors in high school, I would say that it was pretty one-sided."

She shrugged. "Things change," she commented as she stood up and headed for the door. "See you at supper."

Paul had seen her smile to herself and knew that she thought she had planted an important seed.

That night, Maggie had invited more than the usual gang for supper, so the table was full. Several conversations flowed at once, and Paul was aware of Rachel's interest in the one he was having with Sara.

"You've done enough for one day," Paul told Maggie and Sara when they started to clear the table. "Go, sit. Rachel and I have got this."

As they worked together, he waited for her next foray into matchmaking. He didn't have to wait for long.

"You and Sara are a good match," Rachel observed as the two of them finished wiping the dishes. "You look good together."

"Well, that's certainly reason enough to fall madly in love," he replied soberly as if he might actually consider such a thing.

"You know what I mean."

"Not really. Hopefully it takes more than looking good together to make a match."

Rachel sighed heavily. "You should give this thing a chance, you know. You and Sara both. I don't know which of you is the more stubborn."

"Rachel, whatever might have been between your sister and me is long gone—for each of us. We're different people."

"You have a lot in common."

"Why are you so intent on this? I would think the last thing you'd want for either of your sisters is to get mixed up with a nonbeliever like me."

"Maybe Sara would be better equipped to bring you back to your faith. After all, you're both practical types who look at the world through clear rather than rose-colored glasses."

"I wasn't aware that I had asked for help finding anything—especially not my faith."

Rachel shrugged. "You should give it some serious thought, is all I'm saying. Sara could help. You two could be really good for each other."

She was frustrated by the lack of any real progress in her attempts to throw the two of them together. She couldn't decide if it was because of Paul's indifference to her sister or to his spiritual soul. The truth was she had come to like Paul and she really wanted the best for him. He was a decent man who deserved happiness and contentment in his life. Down to her bones, Rachel felt that he could never be truly happy until he resolved his own self-imposed estrangement from anything spiritual and found somebody who could be there for him while he followed his dreams.

She didn't fare much better when she decided to bring the subject up with Sara later that night. In fact, her sister laughed at her.

"Rachel, stop matchmaking. You've got plenty to occupy you. Paul McCoy and I are friends, and that's pretty much all we'll ever be. He's not my type. More to the point—I'm not his type, either."

"But you're exactly alike," Rachel blurted. "I mean...you know. You both like things neat and organized. You're both serious and studious. You're..."

"Rach, did it ever occur to you that maybe what I want in a relationship is what I'm missing in myself? The fun, the spontaneity. Someone who would sweep me off my feet and be completely and impossibly romantic." She closed her eyes and sighed. Then she immediately opened them and went back to grading papers. "That does not describe Paul McCoy."

"What if he likes you? I mean, are you going to break his heart twice?"

"Paul?" She laughed. "Rach, honey, this isn't high school. We've moved on. We're very different people."

"Well, yeah, he said the same thing, but..."

"Besides, Paul isn't staying in Smokey Forge. One day he'll head back to Chicago or to some other big hospital where he can pursue his career." She reached over and patted Rachel's hand. "You really have to stop trying to rescue everybody you meet, Rach. Believe it or not, some of us are quite happy with the way our life is going, and I'm pretty sure Paul is one of those people."

*Maybe so,* Rachel thought, *but he sure does frown a lot for somebody who's supposedly happy and content.*

"You've known these people your whole life," Doc reminded Paul in a conversation one afternoon.

"What's up, Doc?" Rachel asked with a grin when she popped into the clinic. She had stopped by to see if Paul had made any progress on his research.

"My son has turned shy on me," Doc reported with a hint of exasperation.

"I'm just not as comfortable as..."

Doc heaved a sigh and ran his hands through what was left of his snow-white hair. "You have no trouble bothering people with your questions about this parasite. Now I want you to do some actual doctoring and..." He paused, composing himself. "Look, son, we're talking about C. R. Snodgrass, for heaven's sake. You played on the basketball team with the man. The two of you were best buddies."

"And I haven't seen him in over twenty years," Paul replied reasonably.

Rachel looked from father to son and back again. "Paul's a little skittish about actually calling on folks up in the hollers, huh?"

Doc nodded. "You'd think a man who can walk down the mean streets of Chicago could…"

"I could go with him," Rachel volunteered. "Is it Emma? Her time?"

Doc shook his head. "Soon. I just thought it would be good experience for Paul to get out there before there's something big like Emma delivering on the kitchen table because nobody's there to bring her into town. I mean, half my practice is out there, not here." He turned his attention to Paul. "Look, son, I know you want to help your friend with his research, but these folks right here need you, too."

Paul cleared his throat, drawing their attention. "The idea of making a house call is a little intimidating."

"And?" Rachel asked.

"And what?"

"And what are you going to do about it?" she asked, then proceeded to answer her own question. "The way I see it, you have two choices. One, you can sit here all safe and warm inside this clinic and wait for them to come down the mountain, which they won't. That, by the way, has never been your style. Or, two, instead of scooping up little test tubes of water looking for a bug that nobody's seen hide nor hair of for weeks, you can use your God-given talent for healing people who are really in need."

As usual, her assumption that his gift was divinely given rankled. "I didn't see God when I was pulling those all-nighters in med school or working double shifts as an intern and resident," he commented with a frown.

"Clearly, you weren't paying attention," she retorted. "Who do you think helped keep you awake and alert?"

He had quickly learned that the only way to get her off the subject was to change it. "These people are different. They know Dad. They think they know me."

"Probably better than he knows himself," Rachel muttered to Doc.

"Yeah. He's spent too much time away from home," Doc agreed.

"Didn't Emma have some symptoms awhile back that might have been the parasite?" Rachel asked Doc, knowing full well that this would definitely get Paul's attention.

"That's right. Well, that in itself is reason enough for him to go up there."

"Did someone leave the room?" Paul asked, looking around, "because I'm pretty sure that I'm still here."

Doc laughed. "If you have half a brain, son, you'll accept this young woman's offer to go along with you. She can smooth the way for you. She can do the talking and you can do the doctoring."

"She can talk, all right," Paul said as he pricked Rachel's finger to draw the blood sample he needed.

"Ouch," she protested. "You enjoyed that."

He permitted himself a hint of a smile and then gave her his wide-eyed attention. "Oh, did I hurt you?"

"We're going to see Emma, so get that through that stubborn head of yours," she informed him as she pulled her hand away and sucked on the wounded finger.

"Tough lady," Doc commented, and as he left the room he was chuckling.

Rachel stood up. "So, are you going or not?"

Paul stared at her. "You mean *now?*" He glanced at his watch. "It's pretty late."

She laughed. "It's just past four." She turned to get her coat and made muffled clucking sounds under her breath.

"I am *not* chicken," he assured her.

"Then come on," she urged and held the door for him. "I'll drive."

# Chapter Four

C.R. had not changed at all. He was still the same easygoing guy Paul remembered. Five minutes after they started to talk, Paul felt immediately at ease.

"Wanna take some shots?" C.R. asked, nodding toward the makeshift basketball goal he'd attached to the side of his ramshackle barn.

"You sure that thing will hold up?"

C.R. grinned. "You talkin' about the basket or the barn?"

As they took turns shooting the ball, they caught up on what had been happening since they last saw each other. C.R. had served in Operation Desert Storm, and that opened the door for Paul to talk to him about Kosovo. For the first time since leaving there, he felt as if someone truly understood what he'd experienced.

Emma insisted on making supper for them. Paul watched how easily she and Rachel moved around the kitchen, talking, laughing, tending to the four young children who crowded in and out of the small room. Rachel was good with the children, and he suddenly wished he'd taken her up on her offer to come inside the school. Not to visit Sara, but to observe Rachel teaching.

Emma was well into her eighth month, but she barely looked old enough to be a mother once much less five times. The kids brought back memories of Kosovo...the camps...Sami.

"You the doctor?"

Paul looked into the upturned face of a very serious ten-year-old.

"Now, Henry, you leave Dr. Paul alone," Emma said.

"It's okay," Paul said and turned his attention to the child. "Yeah, that would be me." He knelt on one knee to be more at the boy's level. "Can I do something for you?"

"Yep. I need some hep."

*"Hep?"*

"That would be *help*," Rachel prompted him quietly as she passed behind him on her way to put the salad on the table.

"What kind of help?"

"I'm working on me a science project, and Teacher says if I can do it the way I'm plannin' I might get to take it to the state competition."

"I'll do what I can."

"After we eat," Emma instructed. "Now, go wash up. You, too, Paul."

Paul was surprised to see that the boy walked with a pronounced limp as he headed down the hall to the bathroom.

"What happened?" he asked C.R. when he was sure Henry was out of earshot.

"Tractor accident last summer. He was visiting my

brother. He fell off the tractor on some uneven ground, and it rolled over his foot."

"Crushed some of his bones real bad," Emma added as she carried steaming bowls of food to the table.

"Surely, the doctors..."

"Paul," Rachel interrupted, indicating that he was getting into a topic that was best left alone.

"No insurance," C.R. said quietly.

"And nobody like Doc who'd have been willing to ignore that, knowing somehow, some day, we'd pay him off," Emma added as she dished up pieces of fried chicken onto a platter C.R. was holding for her.

"Done," Henry announced as he came back down the hall, holding up his clean hands for his mother's inspection. "Your turn," he told Paul.

At supper, Paul questioned Emma about her symptoms. "When you thought you had the flu," he reminded her.

"You mean that it might have been some bug she picked up in the creek water?" C.R. asked after Paul had explained his preliminary theory.

Paul explained to them the research his friend was doing and how he had seen the same parasite in Kosovo.

"I'll take a sample of the creek water back to check, but I don't want you to worry. It's the same creek that flows past the mill, and we've been checking that regularly. In the meantime, boil your water before using it for anything. Just to be safe, okay?"

"Can I show Dr. McCoy my project now?" Henry asked.

"I'd like to see it," Paul added as he and Henry waited for Emma's permission to leave the table.

When Paul saw the plans for the project, he was amazed at the sophistication of the boy's thought process. The two of them spent quite a lot of time examining the model he'd started to build and figuring out other solutions for what the boy was trying to demonstrate. By the time they were ready to leave, Paul had made arrangements for C.R. to stop by the clinic to get some supplies that Henry would need to finish the project.

"I got you this jar of creek water," C.R. said.

"Thanks."

"You don't think the baby's in any danger, do you, Paul?" Emma asked as she cradled her distended stomach.

Paul realized that his talk of parasites had upset her. "Emma, given the fact that your symptoms were very mild and there's been nothing since, I really think both you and the baby are fine. But, tell you what, I'll run the test on this water sample as soon as I get back to town tonight. Then, tomorrow I'll come back and we'll do a full examination of you and the baby. Would that be okay?"

Emma nodded.

C.R. clapped Paul on the back. "Thanks, Doc. We sure would be grateful for your kindness."

It was the first time anybody in town—other than Rachel—had called him *Doc*. Paul found that he liked the sound of it. More than that, he liked the feeling he got when Emma and C.R. looked at him. It was the same look he'd seen people give his father for decades. It was also the look of hope mingled with trust that he'd seen on the faces of the refugees.

Later, in the car on the way home, he felt Rachel watching him, glancing his way from time to time as she negotiated the winding narrow road she must have driven a thousand times.

"You and Emma are good friends," he said, working at conversation, uncomfortable with her for the first time.

"Best of friends," she agreed. "Emma knows me so well. She inspires me."

"*She* inspires *you?*" He chuckled and shook his head. "I would think that with all your talent and then teaching on top of that, well…"

Rachel shrugged. "I write songs about life. Emma lives life—day in and out."

"She's got her hands full with those kids and another on the way." He shook his head.

"You disapprove?"

"It's not my place to approve or disapprove. I'm just saying that…"

"You seemed to enjoy the children in a distant sort of way, especially Henry."

"He reminded me of someone I knew in Kosovo."

"Samir?"

"Sami. Yeah."

She waited for more, but by now she knew he wasn't the type to volunteer much about his own life, especially the part that had taken place in Kosovo.

"Tell me about him."

He shrugged. "There's not much to tell. He got there just a few days before I left. We didn't have long."

"But he touched you—more than any of the others." She waited.

"He's about the same age as Henry, but looks younger—small for his age. Skin and bones."

She drove and waited for him to go on.

"He'd been through so much by the time I met him

and yet he was always so upbeat. And smart...really smart." He fell silent. "A little like Henry," he added as they approached the lights of town.

"You're good with kids," she commented. "You'd make a good teacher." She pulled up next to his car in back of the clinic, deliberately changing the subject to something lighter because they both had things to do and she knew they didn't have the luxury of lingering over conversation.

"I think you Dukes have the teaching profession pretty well sewn up in this town," he replied.

She didn't smile. She looked at him for a long moment. "Paul McCoy," she said finally as she reached across and brushed the hair from his forehead, "you are one unhappy man. I wish you could see the good that you do—the importance of your work. The way you were with C.R. and Emma tonight—so gentle and understanding. I know you feel guilty about leaving Sami and the others behind, but I believe that God had more important work for you here."

He tried to laugh off the comment, but she was too close to recognizing his feelings of guilt. "It's been a long day," he said as he opened the car door and stepped out.

Rachel decided to drop it, but the fact was Paul McCoy was a good doctor and he was good with the people of Smokey Forge. More and more it occurred to her that maybe God had brought him home to stay. He just needed a reason to do that.

"Do you write to Sami or any of the others?"

"Once in a while."

"Would you mind if I added a note the next time you write to Sami?"

"That would be nice. He'd really like that, but I warn

you, the kid is ten going on twenty-five. Don't you dare
send him a picture or he'll tell everybody you're his
girlfriend.''

Rachel laughed. ''I'll write a letter tonight and get it
to you tomorrow, okay?''

Paul nodded. ''You want me to follow you home?''

''Paul, this is Smokey Forge, not Chicago. I'm perfectly safe.'' She waved and drove off toward home.

She realized that in a way she wished that it *was*
Chicago and she did need him to keep her safe.

It was a Saturday morning in late October when Rachel received the call from Todd Mayfield. It was also
the day she realized that without her noticing it, Paul
McCoy had become her best friend. Todd Mayfield was
a talent agent and manager—one of the best in the country music business and he wanted to represent her. The
first person she thought about sharing that news with—
even before Maggie or Sara—was Paul. That surprised
her.

It also surprised Paul when she showed up at the
clinic in the middle of the morning with no appointment.

''You okay?'' He looked up from adding notes to a
patient's file with a worried frown.

''I'm fine. I just got some news and, well, I thought
maybe you'd celebrate with me.''

''Celebrate?'' He blinked and pushed his glasses onto
the top of his head where they were instantly lost in his
thick, unruly hair.

She might have been speaking a foreign language.

''Yeah, you know, like a birthday party?'' She smiled
and thought maybe this hadn't been such a good idea.
Just because she thought of him as her best friend didn't

mean that feeling was anywhere near to being reciprocated.

"It's your birthday?"

"No. That was an example."

He rubbed his eyes, and she saw that he was exhausted.

"Hey, I'm interrupting you," she said as she quickly backed toward the door. "Are you free for supper tonight? Maggie's making chili."

"Yeah, sure, but you didn't come all the way over here to invite me for supper. Now sit down and tell me what's going on." He led her to the straight-backed metal chair, and she sat.

"I got a call from an agent—you know, from Nashville?" She felt suddenly shy about the news. After all, what was the big deal? He was a doctor who did important research and went off to Kosovo to save lives in his spare time. She was talking about a guy who might get her a gig at the state fair.

"And?"

She shrugged. "He's a pretty good agent—good connections. It might lead to something."

He started to grin. "Yeah? What happened to the deal you made with God that it was first place or back to teaching?"

"As I have explained, God doesn't make deals," she reminded him. "But He does send messages, and if we're paying attention, we don't miss them."

"The agent is a message?" Paul was starting to relax and enjoy himself as he always did when he was around Rachel.

"More likely a messenger."

"This is complicated." He was teasing her now.

"Do you want to hear this or not?"

He held up his hands to forestall the force of her irritation, but he did not stop grinning. "So, your big break has come in the person of...?"

"Todd Mayfield. He represents some of the top names in the business." She felt her excitement building. "Paul, he wants to represent *me*."

"Well, of course, he does. Have you heard yourself sing? You're dynamite, lady."

She grinned. "Aw, shucks, Doc, I bet you say that to all your gospel-singing patients."

"So, what should we do to celebrate? How about a picnic?"

"Really? I love picnics," she said shyly.

"Then a picnic it is. Ready?" He took off his lab coat and reached for his leather jacket.

"Today? Now?"

Paul McCoy was almost never given to spontaneity unless it was related to some new theory about his research. On top of that, he would logically assume that the season for picnics had long since passed. "In October?" she asked.

"I think that's the best plan. It's a beautiful day—October or not. It may be one of the last such days before spring, so we should take advantage, don't you think? Live in the moment. Isn't that what Maggie always says? We have something to celebrate, and there's no time like the present."

They stopped for sandwiches and cans of soda. Paul insisted on adding two gooey chocolate caramel brownies to the feast.

"I think the mill is the perfect spot for this particular picnic," he said. "After all, isn't that where you got your start?"

"You're being really terrific, Paul. Thank you for sharing this with me."

"My pleasure."

As they ate she regaled him with Todd Mayfield's impressive history of taking unknowns to the top of their field.

"Sounds like quite a guy."

She nodded. "And he wants to represent me." She stood up and twirled around and around, her arms flung wide, her head back as she sang the words to the heavens. "It's my dream coming true, Paul. All I ever wanted was the chance to try, and now God has decided to give me that."

Paul joined her in the dance, taking her in his arms and waltzing her around the open meadow next to the rushing stream. As they danced she began to sing—a song of thanks, a song of praise, a song of unadulterated joy.

"Oh, Mr. Todd Mayfield knows a good thing when he hears it," Paul said as the dance ended on a soaring note and they collapsed onto the grass breathless with exertion and happiness. "I'm really proud of you, Rachel," he added as he covered her hand with his.

"I couldn't have done it without you." She laughed. "I mean, imagine what might have happened if I hadn't passed out in front of you that first night." She sat cross-legged in front of him and took both his hands in hers. "Life is filled with such wonderful things like that—me passing out, you being there with Doc. I really think God sent you at that exact moment because He knew I needed your friendship in my life."

"You give me far too much credit."

"No, think about it. What if I'd won in Nashville and not passed out. I would have signed a contract and then halfway through the tour, I might have gotten sick again and then there's your friend and his research and you catching on that whatever I had might be the same as what you saw in Kosovo and..."

"Okay. Okay. Glad I could be of help."

They were quiet for a long moment, sitting together in the comfortable silence that only good friends can experience as they ate the gooey brownies and watched the stream rush past.

"I have to get back to the clinic," he said finally.

She rinsed her hands in the rushing stream, scrubbing at the sticky caramel from the brownies that had oozed over them. She used her wet fingers to scrub her mouth and then turned to him. "Thanks for sharing this moment with me. You made it extra special."

He was staring at her with a very strange look on his face.

"You have that deer-in-the-headlights look," she said.

"You just washed your hands in the stream."

She glanced at the stream. "They were sticky."

"And then you wiped your mouth."

"It was sticky, too." She couldn't imagine where he was going with this. "You're making me a little nervous," she said, and tried to laugh, hoping he would laugh, as well.

"Did you ever do that before? I mean, use the water from the stream to wash up?"

"Well, I don't make a habit of it."

"Rachel, that may be how you picked up the parasite."

It seemed impossible. "It was just a few drops, and besides, this water has tested okay for weeks."

"It may not have been this water. Think. Where else

might you have wet your hands or face in untreated water?''

She was prepared to dismiss his theory as far-fetched, and then she remembered something. ''Oh, my heavens,'' she whispered.

''What is it? Tell me.''

''Last summer, I played a revival down in Hogan's Gap. They were doing baptisms in the river there—full immersions. There was this little girl, and she was afraid but she wanted so badly to be baptized.''

''And?''

''I went in with her. I went *under* with her.'' She stared at Paul. ''That could be it, right?''

''Could be—probably is. I'll call down there tomorrow and make sure they test that water.''

''Make sure everybody's okay, too, will you?''

''I promise, and just to be doubly sure, I'm taking a new sample of this creek water with me to test right now. We can't have you getting sick again now that you're on the verge of stardom.''

She laughed with pure joy, her good spirits completely restored.

As they drove back to town, Rachel talked and wrote notes and lists on scraps of paper that she pulled from her bag and her pockets. She told him that she needed to think about taking care of her teaching responsibilities, handing them off to a substitute in case Todd wanted her to go on tour. Then she was on to thinking about her song list. Did she have enough? Should she add some songs by other artists?

Paul laughed. ''Slow down. You don't even know what this guy's going to do for you. There will be plenty of time to plan when you get that first offer.''

"Maybe," she said, but clearly did not believe it for a minute. "On the other hand..."

"You're going to prepare for any contingency?"

She nodded and grinned. "It's the way I operate."

"Is that how you manage to keep all the balls of your life in the air?"

She shrugged.

He laughed. "Go. I'll see you later."

He was still smiling as he put his lab coat on and returned to his work. It was a slow day at the clinic, which meant he had time to make the calls he needed to make to the clinic near Hogan's Gap and to check the water from the mill, as well. He put a slide under the microscope, and what he saw there gave him more pleasure than any lab test he had ever run. The water was clean. Rachel was in no danger.

Rachel could hardly wait for Paul to come for supper. She'd arrived home to find a message to call Todd Mayfield, and now she had even better news to share with Paul.

"Could you just settle down?" Maggie scolded as she tried to work around Rachel. "You're worse than a pesky fly. Here, go set the table." She thrust the flatware and napkins into Rachel's hands and shooed her toward the dining room.

As she set the table, Rachel hummed a new tune that had popped into her head as she walked home from the clinic that afternoon. Nothing could dampen her spirits tonight.

"So, what did this guy have to say when you called him back?" Maggie asked as she brought in a stack of plates and salad bowls and set them on the end of the large dining room table.

"He thinks he might have an opportunity for me to be the opening act for the Wilson Brothers."

Maggie paused and looked at Rachel. She was clearly impressed. "Really?"

Rachel nodded. "I can hardly believe it myself. Can you imagine? I mean, they're like the biggest name on the charts in gospel right now."

"You'd have an audition?"

"Next week in Nashville."

Maggie came around the table and hugged her hard. "Honey, I am prouder of you than I've ever been of anybody in my whole life."

"I don't have it yet," Rachel reminded her.

"Details," Maggie replied, and Rachel noticed that her sister brushed away a tear with the hem of her apron as she hurried to the kitchen. "Who would have thought?" Maggie said softly to herself. "Little Rachel Duke from Smokey Forge, Tennessee."

Rachel couldn't remember when she had felt so completely happy. She glanced out the window for the tenth time, hoping to see Paul's car. Of course, he probably never even heard of the Wilson Brothers.

She hurried to the CD player and after rummaging through her collection, inserted a disc and turned up the volume. The duo's rendition of "Amazing Grace" filled the house and spilled out onto the porch where Rachel went to wait for Paul.

Paul checked the slide three more times before setting it aside. He pulled out three earlier slides and studied them, as well. They had all tested negative for the parasite. He leaned back and thought about the scene at the stream earlier. His heart had been in his throat the minute he'd realized what she'd done. In that moment he had seen yet again how an instant could change everything. If the parasite had been there, she might have been infected again. Not only that, but it would have meant that C.R. and Emma and the kids were also in danger.

At first when she had washed her hands in the stream, he had laughed, teasing her about being such a messy eater. Even as he watched her wipe her mouth with her wet hands, scrubbing off remnants of the caramel that had stuck to her chin, it never occurred to him to stop her. When he realized what she had done, he felt as if he'd been kicked in the stomach.

He consulted an issue of a medical journal Dan had sent him. It contained the first published studies of this type of parasite.

"In some patients...evidence of a susceptibility to sometimes virulent onset of symptoms...especially if exposure to parasite reoccurs..."

He closed the journal and took one more look at the slide. There was no parasite. Rachel would be all right.

"You coming to Maggie's?"

His father stood at the door, and Paul became aware that the clinic was quiet. Ruby had left for the day, and the last patient had been seen and discharged.

"Yeah. Coming," he said, but he put a few more drops of the water sample on a fresh slide and slid it under the microscope. He had to be one hundred percent sure. His father remained standing at the door, watching him.

"Did you find something new?" Doc finally asked, edging a little closer.

Paul glanced up, then stood to offer his father his place. "Here, take a look."

Doc settled his large frame onto the stool and adjusted the microscope. After a long moment he sat back, removed his glasses and pinched the bridge of his nose. "Where's this from?"

"The mill." He told his father about Rachel's exposure to the water.

"It looks clean." Doc was clearly mystified at Paul's intense study of the sample.

"I know, but what if it hadn't been?" He quickly told his father what had happened earlier that afternoon.

Doc nodded. "Why don't I run up to C.R.'s right away? Just because the water is okay down here doesn't necessarily mean we shouldn't test it up there. I'll take them some bottled water, just until we're sure," Doc said. "You should go on to Maggie's."

Paul glanced at the clock. "I know."

"Son, this is good news—Rachel is fine." Doc was mystified by his son's intense expression.

"I know, but what I need to do now is make sure she's in the best possible shape to take advantage of this opportunity. Remember what happened last time?"

"She was just coming off the virus," Doc reminded him.

"I know, but she doesn't take care of herself at all, Dad. This is her big opportunity. This Mayfield guy could offer her the chance to perform all over the state, and she'd say that was fine and still manage to teach her kids and write half a dozen new songs at the same time."

Doc grinned. "That's our Rachel."

"Well, I'm going to make sure she gets her rest, eats right and starts on a regular program of exercise to build her stamina. She neglects herself something terrible."

Doc gave him a strange look. "Are you sure you can work all that into your own schedule? I mean, you've been spending every free minute helping your friend Dan and staying in touch with your colleagues back there in Kosovo. I won't even bring up the fact that we also have patients here who need you. Maybe I should take on Rachel's care."

"I can do it. I have to do it, Dad." He dumped the rest of the creek water in the sink and missed his father's grin. "She's as stubborn as they come, and I can't really see you jogging down the road with her every evening to make sure she sticks to her exercise."

"Well, if you think that's best," Doc said as if he doubted the wisdom of Paul's choice.

"Dad, I have to do this, okay?" Paul replied, his voice filled with urgency. "I promise you that I won't neglect the others, but Rachel—she's important."

"I understand," Doc said and patted his son's shoulder. "You go ahead. I'll be along later after I go up to C.R.'s place."

Paul nodded and headed out the door. Doc stood there watching him go. "You have to do this, all right," he said to himself as he watched Paul rev his car and spin gravel in his haste to get to Rachel. "But it has very little to do with that little girl being your patient, son. I sure hope you wake up to that before it's too late."

# Chapter Five

"Absolutely not. I don't have time for all of that," Rachel declared, and her expression left little room for discussion. "You said yourself that you didn't find any sign of the parasite, and now you're just plain overreacting."

"But, darling," Maggie chided, "if Doc and Paul *both* think that—"

"I have a thousand things to do just to get ready for the audition and that doesn't even begin to address what I'll need to do if the Wilsons decide to let me open for them." She glanced around the room and saw their collective expression of skepticism. "I am in perfect health," she continued and stood up. "Look at me. I've gained back almost all the weight I lost. My nails are healthy. My color is good."

"You're the one who's overreacting," Sara told her. "All Paul is suggesting is that you start doing a little exercise and make a few changes in the way you eat to be sure you are at your best. It's perfectly reasonable."

"Perhaps you can postpone the audition," Maggie

suggested. "They would understand that you've been sick."

"I haven't been sick in weeks, and Todd Mayfield does not *postpone*," Rachel said. "He finds somebody else."

Paul frowned. "This isn't a game, Rachel."

"I know that," she replied, and her tone was serious and calm. "This is my life—my dream. I know perhaps better than any of you what it will take to get ready for this. God will take care of the rest."

"Even God likes to have a little help, honey," Maggie said.

Rachel sighed. They were right. She was overreacting, but when she thought about everything she needed to do, the idea of adding to the list was daunting. "All right, I give up. Tell me what you've got in mind, Dr. McCoy. It's clearly the only way I'm going to have any peace at all."

"It's not going to be a walk in the park," he warned her. "You're going to have to follow the regimen I set for you religiously."

"To coin a phrase," she teased.

"You know what I'm saying. We're talking about regular nutritious meals—not your usual candy bar and diet soda for lunch. We're talking about proper rest." He paused as if trying to collect his thoughts. "Oh, and exercise, of course. Also, it wouldn't be a bad idea if you gave up caffeine."

"You're making this up as you go along, aren't you?"

He ignored that. "You're going to have to make choices. You can't keep burning the candle at both ends—teaching, tutoring, writing your music, rehearsing and running off here and everywhere just because this Mayfield guy says so, understood?'' Paul asked as if the others had left them alone in the room.

''As long as I get to that audition in one piece,'' Rachel replied with equal conviction.

''When is it?''

''A week from tomorrow.''

There was a long beat during which everyone else watched the couple intently.

Paul was the first to blink. ''That doesn't give us much time,'' he finally conceded.

''My point exactly. Do we have a deal?'' Rachel growled like some grizzled politician in a smoky back room. Then she grinned and stuck out her hand for him to shake and seal the bargain.

''I'm going to hound you,'' he warned.

''So what else is new?'' Her hand remained outstretched.

''You're not going to like it,'' he said as he grudgingly accepted her handshake.

''I expect I'll survive,'' she replied. ''On the other hand, I'm not at all sure that *you* will,'' she added softly as she turned away to serve the dessert. ''You've really got to learn to lighten up, Paulie. The fact is some of this is way out of your control.'' She turned to the others. ''Cake, anyone?''

After supper they sat together on the steps of the porch, sipping their coffee and not talking for several minutes, each lost in thought.

''You saw this parasite recur in Kosovo, didn't you? That's why you got so worked up when you thought I might have ingested it today?'' Rachel asked.

''Yeah.''

''Did Sami have this parasite?''

Paul shook his head. ''His mother had it, and his

sisters. He probably had had a mild case, as well, but he had other problems." Paul frowned. "The fact is, Rachel, we just never know. Things can be going along just fine, and all of a sudden everything changes."

"Are you talking about Sami? Something else happened to him, didn't it? That's part of what frightened you today."

"Maybe."

"Tell me more about him, Paul. How did he get to the camp? Why did he of all of them touch you so deeply?" She shifted a little closer to him and placed her hand in his. "I really think you need to tell somebody about what happened that day he came to camp—the whole story."

Paul took her hand and held it and put his other arm around her shoulders. "It was so cold that day. This fine sleety rain had been falling most of the night and into the morning. Bone-chilling rain—you know, the kind where you swear you'll never be able to get warm again? The sky was gray. The landscape was mud. Even the people seemed pale and colorless. It was like some really overstated Hollywood version of the ravages of war."

"And then Sami arrived," she prompted.

Paul chuckled. "The kid was wearing a red flowered dress when he rode into camp on the back of a wagon with his mother, aunt and three sisters. Talk about a bright spot in an otherwise dismal landscape. He jumped off that wagon as soon as he saw me. Kept hold of the side of it as if the driver might take off with his mom and the others. 'You in charge here?' he demanded in perfect English." Paul laughed at the memory.

"He was wearing a dress? The poor kid."

"The crafty kid. The Serbs were taking all the men and older boys from their houses, rounding them up and killing them. Sami saw them take his father, grandfather, uncles and brothers. He figured out that the way to stay alive was to pretend to be a girl."

"What a clever boy, but how horrible—he's just a child."

"As soon as I introduced myself as the doctor in charge, he motioned his mother and the others over to me. 'They need help,' he said and then he collapsed."

"He must have been exhausted."

Paul was very quiet for a long moment. "He'd been injured by a land mine," he said softly.

Rachel gasped and turned to face him. "No," she whispered.

"One of his little sisters had wandered off into this field, chasing some butterfly or something. Sami had gone after her, knowing there were probably land mines. He made it all the way to her and brought her out, then he tripped on the skirt of that red dress and fell over, triggering a mine. It had happened just minutes before they reached camp. I couldn't figure out why the aunt and the driver of the wagon were so agitated, but only Sami spoke English."

"But he made it. He's alive."

Paul nodded. "He's alive, although by all rights he shouldn't be. When we cut that dress off him..." He shuddered at the memory, then took a deep breath and went on. "The wagon driver had done a pretty good job of bandaging him up, which had stopped the bleeding. We got him on the operating table and did what we could."

"I'm sure you did everything possible," she assured him.

"We had to take off one leg at the knee. The other leg is still all there, but pretty scarred up. The kid won't play soccer again, that's for sure." He delivered this startling news in a monotone that told Rachel more than anything else how much he blamed himself for not being able to do more.

"What about his family?"

"They made it to the camp because of him. You could just see the way things were. Sami had clearly taken charge. His mother was very ill, plus she'd lost everything. Understandably, she'd pretty much withdrawn and given up. The aunt and sisters had no choice but to look to Sami. Part of it was his ability to speak English, but most of it was just pure courage in the face of unspeakable horrors. The kid just refused to allow them to give up." Paul shook his head. "He's one terrific little boy."

"I'm glad you were there for him," Rachel said. "That God brought him to your camp."

Paul grimaced. "Yeah, well, for all the good it did. I saw a lot of children come through that camp, and what I was able to do for any of them was minimal. You find yourself fighting everything—time, the government, the lack of proper medicines and facilities, and of course the general apathy."

"What will happen to him now?"

"His mom didn't make it. She was too far gone physically by the time they reached camp, and she was so depressed. In his latest letter, he told me he and his sisters have been separated from the aunt."

"He's alone, then?"

"Pretty much. Of course, he still has his sisters."

"How old are they?"

"Six and eight."

"He's ten," Rachel said, as if that should matter.

"Almost eleven."

"That's too young for so much responsibility."

"Not in his world, unfortunately," he replied in a voice that seemed to come from far away. "There are a lot of kids like him—kids who have had to grow up too fast. Kids who have seen things that most adults couldn't survive."

"You could bring him here," she said.

Paul stared at her. "It's no use, Rachel. If I could have gotten him out of there, the time to do it was back then. Now…"

"Now he needs rehabilitation. I'm sure he can't get that there. And what about a prosthesis?"

"He's one kid. There are dozens of them just in that one camp."

"You start with one. In time, you can bring others."

"It's hard to get people interested in the world that Sami and his peers inhabit. It's too awful to imagine, and people don't like to think about things they can't fix."

"Well, we have to do something about changing his world, then." Rachel sat up and turned to face him. "I mean it, Paul. We have to get him out of there. We have to get them all out of there."

"It's not that simple, Rachel."

"I know that, but what if you and Doc could expand the services of the clinic—specialize—set up a program to treat injuries? I mean, just think about it. One of the reasons Henry made you think of Sami was his accident. You're drawn to them because they're innocent and they're injured. If you built a place just for the children, we could get grants, we could…"

His head was spinning as the idea rolled off her

tongue as effortlessly as water over brook stones. He raised his hands in mock self-defense and laughed. "Oh, no, you don't, young lady. Right now the best thing you can do is take care of yourself and follow Doctor's orders, okay?"

"But..."

He placed two fingers against her lips to silence her. "No buts, lady. You have more than enough on your plate, and if you want to be at your best for that audition, you'd better live up to your part of our bargain. You take care of that, and I promise you that I'll think about your idea—ideas—okay?"

She nodded, and he took his fingers away from her mouth.

"We're going to start simplifying your life," he continued, "not complicating it with more worries, okay?" He tucked a strand of hair behind her ear.

"He's a little boy, Paul," she said softly. "We have to find a way to help him—to help all of them."

"I know that. You're going to just have to trust me and let me handle finding help for Sami, okay?"

"Okay."

They sat in comfortable silence, enjoying the last remnants of the unseasonably mild October evening. She leaned back and rested her head on his shoulder.

"Paul, I'll bet if you could bring Sami here to live with you, Sara could help. She's really good with kids. Together, the two of you..."

"Rachel?"

"Hmm?"

"One of the things you need to take off your plate permanently?"

"Yeah?"

"Matchmaking. You're really lousy at it, so please give it up."

"But…"

"Now I want you to go to bed." He stood up and offered her his hand to help her up, as well.

She laughed. "It's ten o'clock. I never get to bed before…" She saw his expression and paused. "Time for bed," she said contritely. "Can I at least read?"

"You can read as long as it has nothing to do with school or your music."

"How about the Old Testament?"

"Whatever works," he replied, refusing to rise to her obvious bait. He had no doubt that she was serious in her choice of reading matter, but he also understood that she was testing and teasing him a bit by mentioning it.

"You could read aloud to me," she invited as she dusted off her jeans.

That made him smile. "Now there's something that would definitely put you to sleep." He followed her into the house and said his good-nights to Maggie and Sara. "See that this one gets to bed soon," he directed as he patted Rachel on the shoulder.

"I already have my orders, Doctor," Rachel reminded him.

"I'll expect you to stop by the clinic first thing tomorrow," Paul added. He was all business now. "I want to get some baseline data before finalizing the program I have in mind for you."

"Yes, sir," she replied. "I don't have to be at school until later."

"You aren't coming to school at all," Maggie instructed. "Sara and I have discussed it. You've got just one week to get ready for this audition, and that deserves your complete concentration." She saw that Rachel was about to give her an argument. "I mean it. Between the two of us, we can handle the music. We may not be Nashville stars but we can plunk a guitar and carry a tune when we have to, right, Sara?"

There was no use arguing.

That night, as Rachel lay awake, she started to think about Sami and the other children in the camps. She couldn't get them out of her mind. She envisioned the camps, the terrible conditions she had seen on the news. She thought of the pictures she'd seen of the children who had been stranded there, orphaned or abandoned or ripped from their homes with no future and no place to call home. The expressions on their faces had always tugged at her heart—those brave little terrified faces.

"God, I'm not sure what I can do, but I know You wouldn't have made me aware of Sami unless I'm supposed to do something. Please, help him. He's so very young, and his life has been so terribly hard."

She thought about Paul and imagined him there in the camp walking among the refugees. She thought about the way that he had of striding along, hands thrust into his pockets, shoulders hunched in a manner that seemed to signal a kind of instinct for self-protection. To a stranger, he would appear to be deliberately attempting to keep others at bay. Rachel had seen another side of Paul McCoy. She was pretty sure that Sami had also recognized that deep inside Paul was someone he could count on, someone who cared deeply.

"Henry saw it, too, didn't he?" she whispered

She thought about the night they had spent with Emma and C.R. Paul's trademark reserve had vanished, and the sometimes abrasive exterior that the locals chalked up to too much time spent living in the big city had been missing, as well. The minute he saw Henry limp down that hallway, he'd been totally focused on the boy. She'd seen in his eyes that he wanted—needed—to do something to help. Now she understood that he'd been thinking about Sami that night.

He had treated Henry as an equal—someone to be respected for his unique interests. He had acknowledged the injury but made no big deal of it. It was then that Rachel had fully understood and appreciated that his gift for healing went well beyond simple textbook medicine. He had a talent for listening, an instinct for moving beyond the words to the emotions underneath. Henry, who was painfully shy, had blossomed under Paul's attention. Rachel knew what it had taken for the little boy to muster the courage to talk to Paul at all. She understood that the science project had to be very important for him to have risked such a thing. Most of all, she was captivated by Paul's patience and complete concentration on the child and his needs.

"A person could trust a man like that," she said softly. "And in a world where innocent children get their legs blown off or have tractors roll over them, maybe You sent Paul McCoy to set things right again."

The following morning, when she went downstairs to fix her breakfast, she was comforted by the good feelings she had about Paul and his power to heal.

"Mornin'," she said to Maggie. "Isn't it a fabulous day?"

"Fabulous. Now come sit down and eat. You have to get dressed and get down to the clinic."

"What's this?" Rachel studied the strange-looking food in the bowl Maggie set in front of her.

"Paul stopped by. He wants you to add this to your diet. Roughage. It'll build your strength."

Rachel studied the assortment of grains in the cereal bowl. "It looks like stuff he raked up from some farmer's field." She poked it with a spoon. "What am I supposed to do with this?"

"You can put milk on it and eat it."

"Maybe milk and half a bowl of sugar," Rachel muttered.

"You could have a banana cut up on it. That'll sweeten it and give you potassium, which you probably need." Maggie quickly cut the banana. "I have to get to the school. The heat is stuck on eighty degrees. I expect you to eat every bite of this."

"Yes, ma'am." Rachel took a tiny spoonful of the cereal mixture. "Yuck," she grumbled as she forced it down. "Might as well ask me to eat shredded cardboard."

"It's good for you." Maggie hurried around gathering her books and notes. Just before going out the door, she poured a pale green liquid into a mug and set it on the table. "Green tea," she said. "It's decaffeinated."

"Oh, goody," Rachel said without conviction. She looked at the counter where the coffeemaker usually steamed with freshly made brew. It was still in the same place. It was also empty and recently washed.

"Eat," Maggie commanded as she stopped just shy of leaving the kitchen. "Dr. Paul is waiting."

"I'm eating. I'm eating." As far as Rachel was concerned, Dr. Paul was taking this thing *way* too seriously.

# Chapter Six

The clinic's waiting room was filled.

"Flu," Ruby explained when she saw Rachel's look of surprise. "It's running through town faster than melted butter on a hot ear of corn."

"Rachel, go home," Doc ordered gruffly as he ushered the next coughing and moaning patient into the examining room.

"I had a flu shot," Rachel replied, but Doc was already halfway down the hall, and his attention was on the patient.

"Unfortunately, honey, so did a lot of these folks," Ruby reported. "It's a different strain."

Rachel glanced around the small crowded room and saw a number of waiting patients nod miserably.

"Ruby, I need you to call Mrs. Gaussmore's son and have him come take her home. She's too sick to drive herself. Then I'll—" Paul saw Rachel. "Are you nuts?" he asked in a low tone as he crossed the room in two strides and stood toe to toe with her.

"Actually, I'm here for my appointment—the one *you* made me promise to show up for?"

He ran a hand through his hair and took a deep breath. "Sorry. It's been like this since we opened the doors, and I forgot to call you."

"Well, I'm here and Maggie won't let me help at school so what can I do here?" She started to remove her jean jacket.

He took her by the arm before she could get her jacket off and ushered her out to the street. "You can help by quarantining yourself in your house for a couple of days until the worst of this flu runs its course. You don't want to risk catching anything." He glanced toward the busy clinic. "I have to get back in there. I'll stop by to check on you later, okay?"

"Sure," she said, and could not keep the hint of irritation out of her tone. She started to walk away.

"Wait." He caught up to her. "You understand why I'm concerned about letting you be exposed to the flu, right?"

"I understand."

"Then what's with the attitude?"

She released a heavy sigh. "You are *treating* me like somebody who is sick and fragile. I really hate that."

He blinked, and she knew that her reasoning escaped him.

"I will follow the regimen. I will eat the breakfast cardboard...."

"It's high fiber. You need—"

She placed a restraining hand on his arm. "What I *need*, Dr. Paul, is for you to trust that I'm as invested in being at my best for this audition as you are, but this is not the same thing as Sami or even Henry. You are

not going to fail me in some way, okay? We're going
to do this together—you, me and God, okay?"

"But—"

"You'd better get back inside there before Doc gets
overwhelmed. I'm going home and I'll see you later,
okay?"

He nodded.

She couldn't help herself. She laughed. "Why, Paulie
McCoy, I do believe I have managed to leave you
speechless."

Paul could hear her laughter following him as he
turned and went inside the clinic. How was it, he wondered, that this woman—so young, so inexperienced in
the ways of the world, so innocent—how could this
woman walk around dishing out such wisdom?

Back inside the clinic, he smiled. "Who's next?" he
asked with more enthusiasm then he'd felt all morning.

If Rachel thought Paul had become a fixture in the
Duke household before, she was mistaken. He seemed
to show up at every turn. It started later that same afternoon after Rachel had finished telling Sara about her
confrontation with Paul at the clinic. He knocked at the
back door dressed for a run.

"Do you jog?" he asked when Rachel opened the
door.

"Not if I can walk," she replied.

"It's important to build up your stamina," Sara said
with her usual serious expression. "A workout once a
day could make a difference in the level of your energy,
and that can have a big effect on your performance at
the audition, Rach. You really need to listen to what
Paul is telling you."

Rachel glanced at Paul. "You may have a point. After all, look at what it's done for Paul here." She slowly circled him, ogling his physique in an exaggerated way, and was delighted to see the color rise to his cheeks.

"Are you going to change?" he asked.

"Not likely," she replied with a grin. "Oh, you mean am I going to change clothes so we can proceed with this jogging thing? Well, sure, I'll give it a shot. Do you want something to drink while you wait?"

"That reminds me. Did you drink the green tea I left you?"

Rachel rolled her eyes. "Maggie implied that the tea was her idea." She glanced at Sara, who shrugged her shoulders and gave her a wide-eyed look of innocence. Rachel turned her attention to Paul. "Clearly, my sisters are in cahoots with you."

He did not reply but was obviously still waiting for the answer to his question.

"I drank the tea," she said with a sigh.

"Good girl," Sara said. "You go change while Paul and I whip up a fresh batch."

Rachel groaned and headed upstairs. If there had been any doubt in her mind that Paul and her sister Sara were made for each other, it had disappeared. The man was every bit as overbearing as her sister. Like Sara, he was sure that he always knew best, and he wasn't good at debating the point. Both of them were organized and serious. Once either one of them got focused on some project, they were worse than a hound dog with a fresh bone, never mind that God and other people had different ideas.

She shuddered as she pulled on a pair of stretch pants and an oversize sweatshirt that read Jesus Is Coming— Try To Look Busy. She could hear them downstairs making the tea. She could imagine that Paul would approach the task like Sara did most things in the kitchen—as if it were a science experiment. The two of them deserved each other, whether they were willing to admit it or not.

She pulled her hair high into a ponytail and used it to anchor an old baseball cap that had once belonged to her father.

"Rachel? Are you about ready? We're losing daylight."

"We're not making a movie here," she said under her breath as she squatted and searched under her bed for the mate to her running shoe. "Coming." *No shoe.*

Then she remembered and ran downstairs, one shoe on.

"Were you planning to hop or run?" Sara asked.

"Cute. Last time I wore these I stepped in a big ol' puddle and had to wash the one shoe." She fished it out of the laundry basket and held it up triumphantly.

Paul stared at the found shoe. "You didn't wash both shoes?"

"Only this one was dirty," she answered, and as she laced it up she missed his look of total bewilderment.

"Ready?" she asked as she jogged in place.

"Yes, but you need to warm up." He led the way to the back yard, where he demonstrated a series of stretches and warm-up exercises that he clearly expected her to follow.

"I thought we were losing daylight," she reminded him after he began the fourth exercise.

"A sports injury is preventable if you're properly warmed up," he lectured.

She sat on the ground and wrapped one leg over the other yoga style. Then she proceeded to stretch her legs full out into a split and touch her head to either knee. "Can you do that, hotshot?"

"You youngsters are so cocky," he conceded as he held out a hand to help her up.

She grinned and headed off down the path at a run. "Well, come on, Gramps, at least try to keep up."

He caught up to her easily and let her set the pace. She had a nice easy stride, and after several minutes of running showed no sign of tiring.

"What sports did you play in high school?" he asked.

"I tried out for basketball, but was a total klutz. Then somebody mentioned the track team. I decided to give it a shot and absolutely fell in love with running. The idea of competing against a clock was somehow very inspiring."

"You've kept it up?"

"Not really. Life got in the way—teaching, my music, traveling around to the tent and revival meetings in summer."

"You do that—the traveling around to revivals and such part—for the experience of being in front of an audience, I imagine," he said.

She glanced at him, expecting him to be kidding. When she saw that he wasn't, she spoke in slow, measured tones. "I do that, Paul, because God calls me to do that. He gave me a wonderful gift—a talent that can bring comfort to some and inspiration to others. To *not* go would be selfish. It would be like ignoring all the blessings He's given me and mine."

"Rachel, just for the sake of discussion here, what about the fact that He took your parents when you needed them most? What about the fact that He permitted you to be infected by that parasite last summer?

What about all the terrible stuff that *He* lets happen all over the world—to innocents?''

"Now, you listen to me, Paul McCoy, I will not have you blaming God for every terrible thing that happens to people. He gave us free will to make decisions. He also gave everybody else on the planet the same free will. Don't you think that sometimes somebody else's bad decision—like the guy who decided to have one more beer and then get behind the wheel of his pickup and slam it into my parents' car—is going to spill over on a lot of innocent people?''

Now she was breathing hard. Paul couldn't decide if it was the exertion of the run or the breath it took to deliver that sentence. "I thought that was the point. I thought the Big Guy's job was supposed to be watching over people.''

"The *Big Guy* does watch over people—even you. I imagine for His own amusement, He occasionally lets you run off at the mouth like you've just been doing, instead of zapping you with a bolt of lightning like you probably deserve.''

"Aha, so you do believe He punishes,'' Paul said with a smug smile.

"He reprimands and reminds. Occasionally, He has to slug a person in the face to get that person's attention. Personally, I'm waiting for that to happen to you.''

"You are a strange bird.''

"Could come any day now, the way I see it. You'd better be watching over your shoulder,'' she warned and sprinted ahead of him, her ponytail swaying from side to side in rhythm to her effortless pace.

One afternoon later that week, during what had become their daily run, there was little conversation. Rachel was absorbed in thinking about the audition, and who knew what Paul was puzzling over. All she could tell was that he seemed more agitated than usual.

"How are things at the clinic?" she asked.

"Okay."

"Are you still swamped with flu patients?"

"Not really."

Rachel glanced at him. He seemed oblivious to her presence, much less her attempts at conversation.

"And how was your day, Rachel?" she asked herself. "Well, let's see, right after I force-fed myself my usual shredded cardboard for breakfast and washed it down with about a gallon of that tasteless-might-as-well-drink-water tea, I got a phone call," she replied taking the other side of the conversation.

She waited a beat to let him jump into the conversation. He didn't. "And who called?" she asked herself. "Todd. You know, Todd Mayfield, my agent?"

Paul grunted, but he was still completely focused on his own thoughts.

"And what did Todd want?" she continued. "Oh, he just said that if the audition is a success then I'll be leaving on tour in November. The Wilson Brothers are doing a holiday tour throughout the Southwest, and I would be the opening act. But the best part is that he wants to marry me—the sooner the better."

"That's nice," Paul said.

She stopped running and waited for him to notice. Half a block down the street he seemed to realize that she wasn't there. He turned and jogged back. "What's the matter? Are you having pain? Weakness?"

"I'm *talking to you*," she said, hands on her hips.

"I know. I heard you. Todd, the audition, a possible

tour. Todd's getting married. It's nice.'' He waited, looking at her, clearly confused about what all this had to do with her interrupting their run.

"I said Todd wanted to marry me.''

He blinked as he took that in. "Seriously? You don't even know each other, do you? I mean, I really wouldn't advise—''

"I threw that in there to see if you were paying attention,'' she said. "Todd is already married with four kids and a grandchild on the way. He's not exactly my type.''

"Why would you say that then? I mean, about him wanting to marry you?''

"I was testing you to see if you were listening.''

"I heard you.''

"Well, I don't know how they do it up in Chicago, but down here the normal conversation between two people actually involves both people. There's a comment and then a response and most of the time that does not come from the same person, get it?''

"I'm a little distracted.''

She started to jog slowly again, waiting for him to come alongside. "That's a start. Why are you distracted—that is, more than you usually are?''

"It's nothing for you to worry about.''

"That wasn't the question.''

"Really, it's nothing,'' he insisted.

She stopped running again, and this time she sat down in the middle of the road. "I'm not moving until you tell me, and this is a really dark road once night comes, and there's that curve up there. A car or truck comes barreling around the bend, I haven't got a prayer, and it'll be your fault.''

He laughed in spite of his lousy mood. "You do have this way of getting my attention," he admitted.

"What are friends for? Come on, talk," she ordered, crossing her arms and legs as if she were prepared to follow through on her threat.

He pulled out the water bottle he carried and offered it to her. She took a long drink, and he followed suit. "It's just that…well, there's Dad, for one thing."

Satisfied that he was indeed going to confide in her, she got up, and they resumed their run. "Doc? What about him?"

"I hadn't realized that with age he's gotten pretty set in his ways. I made a couple of changes in the way Ruby does things at the clinic—not major things, mind you, just stuff that will make the office run more efficiently, and then I was trying to add some preventive health education stuff to the program."

"That sounds like a good idea."

"Yeah, well, then I started thinking about what you said the other day. Maybe we could expand the clinic—maybe even think about setting up that special program for kids who have been injured in some way. I know that it all requires big bucks and obviously we don't have that. But when I try to talk to Dad about it and about grants, he says he doesn't have time for such things."

"He's got a point. I mean he's always been a one-man show, and now that the town has grown he must be working overtime just to keep up. How's he going to specialize when he's already taking care of everybody in town?"

Paul nodded. "But then, what happens to a kid from a family who can't really afford specialized care? You know, like Henry. Dad's a talented physician, but he could hardly have handled the kind of care Henry would have needed following that accident, no matter what C.R. and Emma think.''

"Henry's accident wasn't something they could have prevented, Paul. They weren't even there.''

"I'm not blaming them, but if they had had the proper services available here, maybe Henry's foot could have been repaired. I just wish…''

"What?'' She felt as if she needed to hold her breath—as if she were at the brink of some wonderful discovery for Paul.

"Nothing. I came here to help Dad find somebody to bring into the clinic, but if we could help a kid like Henry—and there are dozens of farm accidents, not to mention hunting accidents every year just in this area alone. I'd like to do something about that, Rachel. You made me realize that this is not all that different than what I saw overseas. They are children and they need help no matter where they are.''

"Did you tell Doc that?''

"Not really, but how can I? It just adds to everything he's already doing. He wants to cut back, Rachel, not add more.''

"Maybe he's just afraid that you'll get caught up in trying to help him build a program here and lose sight of your own dreams of getting back to Chicago and your own career. Parents worry about that sort of thing sometimes.''

It was his turn to stop running and look at her in surprise. It had never occurred to him that while he'd been mulling over the idea that maybe staying in Smokey Forge wouldn't be so bad, his dad had assumed that his plan was still to leave as soon as possible. "You constantly amaze me, Rachel. I mean that's an incredibly insightful thing to say and especially coming from someone who has gone through most of your life without benefit of parents."

"Ah, but I had Doc and your mom while she was alive. And of course, I had Maggie and Sara—talk about surrogate mothers!"

They began to run again.

"You know, Paul, this is the first time since you've been back that I've heard you talk about your dreams. You've talked about Dan and his research, and of course you've been there for me through everything, but nothing for yourself. If anything were possible, what would you do—to help kids like Henry?"

His face lit with excitement. "I was thinking about a mobile clinic—you know, take the medicine and therapy to them? Maybe one day, we *could* expand the clinic to include a state-of-the-art rehabilitation center—attract the best therapists, build it into a program respected throughout the region, maybe even the nation."

"Now, *that* sounds expensive."

"It would be, but if we could find the funding, we could do amazing things."

"Like what? If you had the funding, what would you do?"

He sighed heavily. "What *wouldn't* I do? These kids—regardless of where they live—are innocent victims of the dangers of the world. The kids in Chicago had to be afraid all the time of drive-by shootings. The kids in Kosovo had the land mines to contend with—that's assuming they made it out of the villages in one piece. The kids here are safer, but they are still around dangerous stuff, like farm equipment and hunting rifles. It's a wonder any of them make it to adulthood.''

"Your program would give them a better chance,'' she reminded him gently.

"We can't prevent the accidents, necessarily. But we could help them rehabilitate themselves. We could give them a better chance at recovering.''

"So, this mobile clinic would be some kind of van with equipment that would travel up and down the hills sort of like a library bookmobile?''

He grinned. "Something like that. Sounds like a pipe dream, huh?''

"Not at all. I think it sounds terrific. I mean, wouldn't it be cool if you could bring Sami over here, get him out of the horrible place, give him his chance? Wouldn't that be incredible?''

He laughed. "You just never see the glass half-empty, do you?''

"That's the gift of faith, Paul. All things are possible—you just have to find the right path.'' She turned onto a narrow cow path that ran down the hill toward the millstream. "Like this one,'' she called happily. "Come on. Last one to the stream has to come to church with me next Sunday.''

Once again, she had succeeded in breaking his mood and getting him to laugh. "No fair,'' he shouted as he took off, running hard, pushing to pass her. "And if I win,'' he called over his shoulder, "then the last one there owes the winner dinner and a movie.''

"Going to church will get you a lot closer to realizing your dream than dinner and a movie,'' she yelled and ran after him.

"Yeah? Well, what if my dream at the moment is a date with you?" He kept running.

She stopped and stared after him in dumbfounded surprise and then heard his laughter. There was no way she could catch him now, and he knew it.

"You'll do anything to win," she called after him. The idea that Paul McCoy might be interested in a date with her *was* ridiculous, wasn't it?

# Chapter Seven

"**Y**ou have got to help me," Rachel whispered into the phone two days later.

"Rachel? I can barely hear you," Paul said. "Are you feeling ill?" His voice reflected his usual concern.

"I'm fine. It's just that Maggie and Sara have both decided they need to come with me for the audition."

"That's nice," Paul replied.

"It's a nightmare," Rachel screeched hoarsely. "You know how they are. Maggie will be in full-blown nurturing mode, and Sara—well, Sara will be her usual I-know-better-than-you-do self. I can't *do* this."

"And I can help you by?"

"Say you'll go with me for the audition. *Please.* You don't actually have to go, but just let them think you'll be there to watch over me and…"

"Slow down." He covered a chuckle with a cough.

"Stop laughing. This is serious. Surely you of all people know how they can be. You grew up with them."

"I was blinded by Sara's beauty, remember?"

"Well, get unblinded for a minute and help me out here or, for the rest of your born days, carry around the guilt of my failed audition with the hottest act in gospel." She gripped the phone. "At least have the common courtesy to stop laughing," she ordered, "and help me get out of this mess. The audition is the day after tomorrow."

"I'll go."

"The least you could..."

"I said I'll do it."

"Oh." She paused. "You know, you don't really have to."

"Okay. I'll stay here and work."

"No," she protested and then spoke more softly as she caught Maggie's curious glance from the kitchen. "I mean, I just..."

"Why are you whispering?" he asked in an exaggerated whisper.

"Because unlike you big-city types, we only have one phone in this house, and it sits here in the middle of the downstairs hallway where anyone might wander by."

She could hear the hint of barely suppressed laughter in his voice as he spoke normally. "Okay, what time do we need to leave? What time's the audition?"

"Four in the afternoon."

"Okay, we'll leave early. Take our time so you can relax."

"You mean it?"

"Sure. It'll be fun."

"You don't *do* fun, Paul," she said suspiciously.

There was a pause. "Okay. I was going to be in Nashville Saturday anyway to see a friend at the university. He's done some work with accident victims—

adults, mostly. We've been planning to get together to share notes."

"You rat. You could have offered to give me a ride all along."

"I beg your pardon," he replied. "Just a minute ago I was saving you from the fate of spending one of the most important days of your life under the thumbs of your well-intentioned but overbearing sisters."

"Well, when you put it that way, I guess I could hitch a ride with you…as long as you're going anyway."

This time he made no attempt to disguise his mirth. He laughed out loud, and she realized how much she had come to enjoy the sound of it. "You're welcome. Get a good night's sleep, songbird."

"We'll be back before midnight," Rachel promised her sisters as Paul drove slowly away from the house two days later.

"But you'll call the minute you know," Maggie shouted as Paul pulled the car out of the driveway.

"Yes, okay. I'll call," Rachel promised and waved.

"Could you get all the way in the car and fasten that seat belt, please?" Paul instructed. "You'd think you were going on a six-month safari, not a simple day trip to Nashville."

"There is nothing *simple* about this," Rachel replied testily as she flung herself into the seat and tried without success to fasten the seat belt. "I don't think I'm ready. I should have prepared another selection—something more upbeat. They're going to think I'm a rank amateur."

"Here," Paul said as he steered with one hand and deftly clicked the seat belt into place. "Take a deep breath. Go on. Deep." He demonstrated. "Now, let it out slowly."

"It makes me light-headed."

"Good. It's working. Again." He drew in a long breath and blew it slowly out through his open lips.

"You are seriously weird," she said, but she did as he instructed and found she was indeed feeling better.

"Okay, now what?"

"Warm up," he instructed.

"Excuse me?"

"Whatever it is that you do—scales, la-las. You know, warm up the pipes."

She giggled.

"Shall I demonstrate?"

"You're serious? You sing?"

"I happen to have been in the choir at school for at least a week, young lady, before I realized they actually expected me to rehearse." He started to hum and then sing an off-key version of "Coming 'Round the Mountain." "Feel free to join in."

"That's really terrible."

He stopped singing and gave her a pained look. "I'm crushed."

They rode along in comfortable silence. She dozed. He turned the radio on low and enjoyed the passing scenery. Halfway there he pulled into the parking lot of a roadside coffee shop.

"Are we there yet?" she asked sleepily as she sat up and looked around.

"No. I just thought we'd take a short break. How about some green tea?" He grinned and held up a plastic sandwich bag containing tea bags. "Maggie sent them along. She also instructed me to make sure you had yours with honey."

"She's impossible," Rachel replied, but she said it with a smile, and he knew that she was touched by the caring gesture.

Once they were in the coffee shop, she grew uncustomarily quiet.

"Are you still nervous?" he asked.

She shrugged. "A little. It's probably normal, don't you think?"

He pretended to consider that. "Well, now, let's analyze that. Were you nervous that night at the talent show?"

"Well, of course."

"Are you nervous when you sing at church or at a revival?"

"No."

He stroked his chin as if he had suddenly grown a beard. "Then here's what I'm thinking. If you pretend that you're back home singing at church, you'll be fine."

"Thank you, Dr. McCoy."

"No problem. Now, drink your tea and let's talk about that date you owe me."

"You used that to cheat, and you know it," she protested.

"I did not. It was a bona fide offer, a bet that you lost and one that I fully expect to collect on. How about Saturday?"

"This is Saturday," she reminded him.

"As in next week."

"We'll see."

"Ah, the lady is playing coy with me." He twirled an imaginary mustache. "Well, I always collect on my bets, Miss Duke, so don't try to get out of this one."

"You're playing mind games," she replied and drank the rest of her tea.

He leaned back and studied her. "Maybe. Maybe not. I did make you forget about being nervous for five minutes, didn't I?"

She smiled. "Yeah. You did. Thanks."

When they reached the outskirts of the city, she began to fidget.

"You're going to do fine," he assured her.

"I'm more nervous than I would have imagined," she confessed.

"Maybe because it means so much to you?"

"Yeah, maybe."

He parked in front of the theater, and they both stepped out of the car. He offered to come in with her, but she refused. "I have to do this on my own. Can you understand that?"

"More than you know."

"You go see your friend and talk shop. I've got the number, and I'll call you the minute it's over."

"Sounds like a plan."

She started to walk away, her guitar case in one hand, a garment bag with her dress for the audition in the other.

"Hey," he called.

She stopped and looked back.

He walked the few yards to her and kissed her gently on the forehead. "You're very, very talented, Rachel. If you don't get it, it won't have anything to do with who you are or your talent, okay?"

"Thank you."

"You're welcome. Now, go knock 'em dead, songbird." He gave her a light tap on her backside.

\* \* \*

Paul had stopped listening to his friend's explanation of the research he was conducting and started checking his watch. It was nearly six, and there had been no call. Was that a good sign?

Ten minutes later, the phone finally rang as if he had somehow willed it to happen. His friend answered and handed him the receiver.

"Hi."

He could tell nothing from her voice.

"Should I come get you?" he asked.

"Yeah. I'm pretty hungry. Did you guys eat yet?"

They were talking about the mundane. She hadn't gotten it. "Rachel, I'm…"

"'Cause the Wilsons would like us to join them for some of the best barbecue in Nashville."

"Really?"

"Yeah. You don't mind, do you? They want to talk about the tour, and I told them I had to get back tonight. They're cool with that, but they—"

"You got it."

She started to laugh, and it was music to his ears. "Well, yeah, if I can manage to put together an opening act between now and when we leave on tour in November."

"You got it. Oh, Rach, that's really terrific." He didn't stop to analyze why he didn't feel all that happy at hearing the news. After all, it was what she wanted— what he wanted for her. "Congratulations. I'll leave right now."

It was a wonderful evening for Rachel. Paul could see that traveling with the Wilsons would be a family affair. Ezra Wilson's wife was part of the crew, as were several other relatives. They were professionals who knew how to have some fun. But he had some doubts about Todd Mayfield.

He didn't like the way Mayfield looked at Rachel, as if she were a commodity to be marketed like breakfast cereal or the latest hot toy for kids. He didn't like the way he kept talking about changing her clothes and her hair to give her what he called more pizzazz. If there was one thing Rachel had, it was genuine pizzazz. The woman lit up a room. Mayfield talked in terms of promotions and referred to her as a potentially hot property. It was all Paul could do not to punch the guy in the nose.

Rachel seemed enthralled by it all. She listened carefully to everything her new manager told her. She hung on every story the Wilsons told of life on the road. Her eyes sparkled with anticipation. She blushed when one of the Wilson brothers complimented her on her talent for songwriting.

"Honey, it's one thing to sing 'em," Ezra Wilson told her. "Writin' 'em is a whole different ball game, and you write real good stuff, little lady."

"We were thinking maybe you might put your mind to writing something we could all do together," Jonah Wilson added.

"A finale," Todd said with glee. "A grand finale."

Rachel was incredulous. "You want me to write a song for you?" She looked at each of the brothers in turn.

"Yep, and sing it right along with us. How about a holiday song since it's a holiday tour?" Jonah suggested.

Rachel was in shock. "This can't be really happening," she said with a shy shake of her head. "I mean, me sitting here at supper with the Wilson Brothers just like…''

"Ordinary folks, honey," Ezra's wife, Pearl, told her. "That's all we are. We happen to make our living singing songs—spreading the good news. It's not that different from a traveling preacher."

"Except when's the last time you heard of a traveling preacher being paid six figures to do a tour?" Todd gloated.

"It's God's work and God's will, Todd, and don't you be forgettin' that," Pearl said sternly, and Paul saw that she didn't like Todd Mayfield all that much, either.

In the car on the way back to Smokey Forge, he listened to Rachel describe every detail of the audition—what everyone said, how they looked, what they asked and how she answered. He realized that in spite of her joy, he couldn't shake a concern that she wasn't really ready for the bright lights of big-time show business.

"You know, it's not going to be all seashells and balloons out there," he said and regretted it the moment the words were out of his mouth. This was her night. He shouldn't spoil it.

"Well, of course. There are rough spots in any job. I know it can get lonesome out there on the road, but I'm going to be lucky to have Pearl and the others— she's a lot like Maggie, don't you think?"

Paul smiled. "Yeah, she is."

"And Ezra reminds me a little of Doc—same sense of humor, and he just can't help playing the big protector to everybody else. Jonah's a foot taller than he is, but Ezra still treats him like his baby brother."

"I thought you didn't like that sort of thing."

She glanced at him. "What are you doing?" she asked, and her voice had lost all of its enthusiasm.

"Nothing. What do you mean?" But he knew what she meant. He was throwing a huge wet blanket on her high spirits, and he couldn't for the life of him figure out why. "I'm sorry," he said honestly.

"Aren't you happy for me? I thought you, of all people…"

"I'm really happy for you. I'm thrilled for you."

"But?"

He covered her hand with his and squeezed it. "Don't mind me. I am truly happy for you."

They drove for a while in silence through the dark night.

"I'm an insensitive idiot," she said quietly after several minutes. "Here I've been going on and on about my day and I never even asked about your meeting with your friend at the university. What did you find out?"

"There's not much to tell. We compared notes. I checked out some research he's doing."

"On injuries from accidents?"

"Yeah. He's started to do some preliminary research for an international organization on injuries from land mines."

"Not in this country?"

"No. Overseas. The Middle East, mostly. He's on the verge of getting some major grant dollars. He might be interested in working with me on building a rehab program."

He turned off the interstate and headed for Smokey Forge. "Hey, why are we discussing all this serious and depressing stuff? You have made a major step forward in your career today. I am so proud of you, songbird."

She sighed and stretched. "It is pretty awesome, isn't it?"

"Yeah, who would have thought—me driving around with a real live country music star."

She giggled and punched his arm, but he could tell that he had succeeded in returning her thoughts to the wonder of the day just past.

The time raced by, and Rachel had never been busier or happier. She worked with Todd Mayfield and his staff to develop and perfect her opening act. She rehearsed for hours and accepted every opportunity to try out her songs in front of an audience. Maggie and Sara recruited a college senior doing his student teaching to double as the music teacher for the rest of the term.

Rachel spent as much time as possible with Paul, relying on him for advice on her selection of songs, her choice of wardrobe and how to conduct herself in the interview. Even though Paul was as busy as she was, he and Doc still came for supper at the farm several times a week, and he called a couple of times a day.

"It's like a dream coming true in fast forward," she said one day when he called after she'd had a particularly exhilarating rehearsal.

"You're the one who's working to make it all happen," he reminded her. "Don't forget that."

"Gee, wonder what else or *who* else might be responsible."

He was silent.

"Prayer works, my friend," she said happily. "You should give it a try. What if I told you it could help you find a way to get the money you need for the mobile unit? Think about it. Now, hang up the phone so I can get my beauty rest."

Beauty rest was the last thing she needed, he thought.

"Tomorrow's the big day." The closer the time came for her to leave, the less he wanted her to go. He told himself that he was just worried about her. She was inexperienced, and he would hate to see the tour end up being less than she had expected.

"Yeah. It's pretty amazing."

"The time will go really fast," he said, even as he thought how interminable it was going to seem not seeing her for the next two weeks.

"I wish…" She paused.

"More wishes? I thought they had all come true," he teased.

"Yeah, well, I'll miss you."

For a minute, he thought that she might be saying more. *Don't be an idiot,* he thought. *In all the weeks you've known her, there's never been the slightest hint that she views you as anything other than a friend.* "You'll be fine, and there's always the phone."

"It works both ways. I mean, if you need a friend…or something."

"I'll keep that in mind. After all, you still owe me that date, lady."

She laughed, but made no reply.

*McCoy, you're an idiot.* "I'd better let you go and get that rest," he said aloud. "That tour bus will be pulling into town bright and early tomorrow."

She didn't want to hang up.

Neither did he.

"Good night, songbird," he said softly.

She hung up and saw Sara standing in the doorway of the kitchen.

"I'm gonna say this just one more time—you're nuts

for not seriously going after that guy," Rachel said as she passed her sister and headed upstairs.

"Maybe you're the one who should go after him," Sara replied.

Rachel laughed. "Yeah, right. That's really gonna happen." But she couldn't help blushing with pleasure at the thought. Perhaps if she took him up on that date thing, it might lead to something. "On the other hand," she said aloud, "why complicate a perfectly incredible friendship, right, God?"

There were three large buses parked outside the town hall. The bus belonging to Ezra and Pearl was at the front. The bus was awesome. It was outfitted with a full kitchen, which was Maggie's favorite part. She and Sara had both insisted on inspecting the vehicle for themselves. Sara was outside with the driver looking over the tires and the engine.

"Look at this," Maggie whispered excitedly as she ran her hand over the stove and refrigerator. "It's incredible and so compact."

"The boys like their home cooking, especially when we're on tour," Pearl said. "Jonah's bus is the same size, but he spends a lot of time riding up here with us. His wife is expecting pretty soon and won't be going with us on this tour. Now, Rachel, honey, this is your space here." She pulled aside an accordion-pleated door and revealed a small sleeping area.

"That's really nice. Thanks." She glanced out the window.

"He'll be here, honey," Maggie assured her.

"It's okay. We said our goodbyes last night." She smiled and turned to Pearl. "It's my friend Paul—you know, the doctor?"

"Oh, he's a cutie, that one," Pearl said, gushing. "Don't let him off the hook, sweetie."

"But he's not...that is, we're just really great friends."

"Uh-huh," Pearl said, and nudged Maggie. "I'll just go be sure the boys are ready to head out." She held the door for Sara, who was just coming to see the interior. "You folks take your time here."

As soon as Pearl left, Maggie held out her arms to Rachel. "My baby sister," she said, her voice choking a little as she hugged Rachel hard.

"It's only for two weeks," Rachel assured her.

"You'll call every night?" Sara added, joining the circle and hugging them both.

Rachel nodded, her eyes misty as she realized that this was really about to happen.

Someone cleared his throat, and she looked over Maggie's shoulder to see Paul standing in the door of the bus.

"I think there are some people out here who'd like to say goodbye," he said.

Rachel went to the door and looked out to see what looked like the whole town gathered in the town square. A sign that read Rachel Duke, Our Very Own Singing Star was stretched across the front of the bank. Her students launched into a song as Doc presented her with a bouquet of flowers. "Break a leg, honey," he said, then looked confused. "Does that work for you concert singers as well as people in the theater?"

Rachel hugged him hard and assured him she accepted all forms of good wishes. She turned her attention to the other townspeople gathered to see her off.

"This is really too much," Rachel cried as she waded

into the crowd and happily accepted the hugs and good wishes of the people she had known all her life.

"All aboard," Todd Mayfield shouted, looking at his watch.

Rachel turned and found herself face to face with Paul. In that instant the words of her sister came back to her. *Why don't you go after him?*

She rejected the thought for a second time as impossible. Paul McCoy had and would always think of her as the kid sister in the Duke family. He might have gotten over his feelings for Sara, but there was nothing to indicate that he had transferred those feelings to her. Not even that ridiculous business about him pretending to want an actual date with her.

"Here," he said, pressing a paper into her hand. "In case you need me. Not that I think anything will go wrong—just a little insurance."

She glanced at the numbers on the paper and then gave him a puzzled look.

"It's my cell phone. If you need me, dial that number, okay? Not that you will—need me, I mean. I assure you that I'm not trying to mother-hen you. But just in case." He folded her fingers over the paper and held on. "You're going to be terrific, Rachel. They're going to love you."

"But?" Rachel knew that Paul would probably always view the world with a heavy dose of skepticism. With Paul, there was always a but.

"But it's a very different world out there. Things aren't always what they seem. People aren't always what they seem to be. I just want you to know you can always call home, okay?"

"Like E.T.?"

He laughed. "Yeah. Like that."

Rachel reached up and hugged him to keep him from seeing the tears that threatened. He was determined to look after her even if it was under the guise of a big brother. He was giving her his blessing in spite of the reservations he had expressed a few nights earlier. "Thank you," she whispered. "Thank you for everything."

He was standing with the others as the bus pulled away, but when she thought about it later, she realized that he was the only one she had really seen. She fingered the paper in her pocket, then thought about the money Sara had insisted on stuffing in her other pocket as she boarded the bus.

Rachel frowned and folded the note. Who was she kidding? She had a crush on the good doctor while he clearly still saw her as somebody in need of care. She'd just have to prove herself to him once and for all. She was a full-grown woman, perfectly capable of making her way in the world. She appreciated everyone's concern—she really did—but she was so tired of being everybody's kid sister. The next time Paul McCoy saw her, he was going to have to recognize that little Rachel Duke was all grown-up.

# Chapter Eight

True to her word, Rachel called home every night. She always called at suppertime, when she knew they would all be there but there wouldn't be a lot of time to talk. She told Maggie that this was the only possible time to call. She was so busy and the shows ran so late and there were pre-show interviews to be done and back-stage guests to be met, not to mention rehearsals.

The truth was that she wasn't ready to share her experiences on the road with them. At first, everything was new and exciting, but that lasted only the first week. By the second, they had settled into a routine that was either boring or exhausting or both. Rachel tried to remain upbeat, but the truth was that being on the road was very different than what she had imagined.

Maggie and Sara plied her with questions, wanting every detail of her adventure. Rachel found that she needed time to digest how she was reacting to what was happening to her—the changes she was experiencing, the ways in which being on tour were different from what she had expected. The more they pushed, the more closemouthed she became. She knew that if she tried to provide details, they would hear in her voice how exhausted she was, how grueling the schedule was.

She wouldn't even have to tell them about the endless boring hours on the bus, trying to catch a nap sitting up or serenaded by the rumble of the tires on the asphalt. They would read between the lines as they always had been able to and they would know. Most of all, they would hear in her voice that she was lonely and homesick in spite of the many kindnesses of the Wilsons.

If Paul had stopped by for supper, he always got on the phone. Fortunately for Rachel, the location of the phone in the Duke house plus the fact that everyone wanted their turn to talk to her made any real conversation impossible. She knew that Paul was concerned. She could hear it in his voice. He, of all of them, would see through her efforts to be upbeat and cheerful. He would know that life on the road was—as he had predicted—not at all what she had expected.

After several rushed phone calls in which Rachel barely seemed to have time to say hello, Paul began to worry. She did not sound like herself. She was enthusiastic and upbeat, but as the days passed it sounded more and more as if she were putting on a performance for all of them. Her tone was too bright, and her laughter sounded forced.

After a week of this, Paul made sure that he would be the last to get on the line with her. The others would have their fill of news by then and drift to the kitchen or living room. Maybe he could really talk to her for a change.

"You sound different," he stated flatly.

"I am different," she agreed with a lightness he would swear she didn't feel. "It's a different life."

She sounded defensive, and that wasn't like her at all.

"How are you?"

"Fine. Great. Oh, a little tired, but we're traveling or setting up for a show or doing a show—the days are really full, you know. It's a normal kind of tired, Paul. I'm not sick again, honest."

He hadn't even been thinking of her physical health, but she had become instantly defensive. He realized that he didn't know how to talk to her over this distance that was both geographical and emotional. "I meant that in a general way, Rach. I know you're in good health."

"Oh." She sighed, then added in that bright, forced tone he had come to dread, "They extended the tour—how about that?"

"That's good. Isn't it?" *I hate it. Come home where you belong.*

She ignored the pointed question. "We've added four shows in Dallas and then two weeks of bookings after that."

"Really?" He tried to fake enthusiasm and knew that he had failed.

"Yeah. I mean, this is all so amazing. Well, I have to go. Tell everyone I'll call tomorrow—same time. See you."

The line hummed, and he slowly hung up the phone.

On the drive home that night, Paul asked his father, "Dad, do you think you could manage on your own for a long weekend?"

"You going down to see Rachel?"

"Yeah. I thought I'd surprise her."

Doc chuckled. "That one sure does know how to get

under a person's skin. Are you going because you're worried about her or because you're finally owning up to the fact that you're sweet on her?''

"She's a good kid, Dad, and maybe under other circumstances..." He shrugged. "The fact is, she has her career and I have mine. The two don't really blend, but we're good friends, and that's more than a lot of people have."

"I see," Doc said slowly. "So you're traveling all the way to Texas because you want to see your good friend?"

Paul sighed. "Yeah. Maybe. I don't know. She sounds completely changed and not for the better."

"Yep, I think you might have a point. She's a little too excited and upbeat when she calls in. It isn't natural talk."

So Doc had heard it, too. Paul breathed a sigh of relief that he wasn't imagining things. "In addition to being my friend, she's also my patient, Dad. I know that physically she's fine, but I promised myself when I left Sami and the others back there in Kosovo that I would never again desert a patient if I didn't have to."

Doc was quiet for a long moment. "I'm sorry I pulled you away from that, son."

As Paul realized how his words must have sounded to his father, he reached over and clumsily grasped the older man's shoulder. "I didn't mean it that way, Dad. I was ready to give up. I was so frustrated by not being able to make a difference for those kids, those people.... The truth is I would have left anyway. Your call just gave me the reason I needed to do it without feeling guilty about it."

"But you do feel guilty."

"Yeah. At the same time I can see that I made the

right choice. I'm glad I came home, Dad. I'm really glad you called.''

"My being lonely wasn't the only reason I called you, son," Doc admitted.

"Why else?"

"I was worried about you. There was nothing in your letters I could put my finger on, but it seemed to me that ever since you left the hospital in Chicago you'd been flopping around like a trout out of water. No direction. No goals. You always knew exactly what you wanted, son, and how to go about getting it."

It was as close to the truth as anyone other than Rachel had come. Paul remained silent.

"Truth is, I've been thinking about that idea you had for a traveling clinic and rehabilitation center for the kids. I reckon we *could* set up a program here. I've done a little checking around. We could get the old abandoned hospital building and fix it up. That would give you the room, and it has a good layout for the center. I also ran into Hank Riddle over there at the dealership, and he might be persuaded to donate a van. Of course, we'd have to raise some money to outfit it, but…"

"How did you know about all of this?"

Doc chuckled. "Well, certainly not from you. Rachel took me out for coffee before she took off on tour. She gets pretty excited about this stuff—mostly because it focuses on the kids. You two have a lot more in common than you may think."

"She's got her own career to manage. Besides, even if I could get the program going, what about you? You can't spare me from the clinic until you find a partner, and face it, nobody is exactly racing down here to operate a small-town practice in the hills of Tennessee."

"I've been thinking about that, too. I was talking to

Sam Doolittle, the hospital administrator over there in Bloomville, last week. He got pretty excited about the idea of our working on something like this together—rotating residents through here. They could give me the help I need. Then we could work through him to make services available to poor kids here in the mountains and maybe also…"

Paul stared at his father. "Dad, I appreciate what you're trying to do here, but…"

Doc ignored him. "Seems to me you'd want to take things a step beyond treating kids in this area. Might even be able to see about bringing some of the worst cases from overseas here."

"The kids from Kosovo?"

"Yeah, I was talking to Sara about this grant stuff. Seems there might be money to bring some of the most needy kids here for treatment. Probably your Sami would qualify—him being an orphan and getting cut up by that land mine."

"You're serious."

"Well, yeah, I am. You seem to have taken to this idea, and I've got to tell you, son, that it's a load off my mind to see you finally get interested in something again. We all knew that it would take a lot more than just being a small-town doctor to keep you happy. If this project gives you a reason to stay, then I'm for doing whatever it takes to make this happen."

Paul couldn't believe what he was hearing. His dad had seemed so set in his ways. Now he was talking about developing a sophisticated program of services that many major hospitals would hesitate to take on. On top of that, he'd already done a great deal of work toward getting the dream on its way.

"You don't have to do this, Dad," Paul said. "I'm going to stay as long as it takes."

"This is no bribe, son. I've been watching you work, listening to your stories, reading the articles. Rachel tells me that you've kind of gotten hooked on treating the mountain folks around here."

Paul smiled. "They remind me of the people in the camps."

"I thought so. Look, son, this thing is something a lot of people need. Rachel's right. There's nothing to say it can't get started right here in Smokey Forge. We may not have the money now but we can get that. What's most important is that we have you here, and you are the person most qualified to build this program. Are you game?"

Paul felt an ember of excitement that had been banked far too long begin to glow deep inside him. His father was offering him the opportunity to make a real difference. More important, his father wanted to help build that project because he believed in Paul and what he could do.

"I'm game," he said as his father pulled the car into the garage.

"Then let's get started, son."

They sat at the kitchen table until well past midnight discussing ideas for the program. Paul was astounded at what his father had already put into motion, including the plan for residents from the hospital his friend Sam Doolittle ran to rotate through the clinic starting immediately.

"It's a temporary solution," Doc said, "but it will free you up to do what you need to do to get this thing off the ground. Besides, I think I just might enjoy playing the professor to these young upstarts."

Paul and his father had never been the demonstrative type. That was more Paul's doing than Doc's. Paul looked at his dad across the kitchen table and saw a man whose devotion and dedication to the science of healing was as undeniable as that of any doctor who had ever lived. "I'm really proud to be your son, Doc," he said, and his voice was husky with emotion.

They were both misty-eyed as they stood up and moved toward each other. "Let's get this thing built, son," Doc said as he pulled Paul hard against his chest and hugged him.

Long after Doc had gone upstairs to bed, Paul sat at the table making notes. He wished he knew how to get in touch with Rachel. He'd like to tell her about his father's surprising move. He'd like to hear the flood of ideas he knew would start to spew out of her like lava from a volcano. He'd like to see the delight in her expression, her eyes lighting up, her radiant smile. Realizing that, he knew that he had another reason for wanting to go to see her. He missed her. Rachel Duke had touched something deep inside him—something he had thought had died there in Kosovo.

"Sweetheart, you hear the reaction as well as I do," Todd Mayfield argued. "The audiences love it when you go a little rock and roll, a little funky. It's time we made some changes—the clothes, the arrangements."

"It's just not my style," Rachel protested as she eyed the costume Todd had thrown across the chair. The demo tape he was playing of a new arrangement to one of her songs pulsated in the small room. She had to raise her voice to be heard.

"Trust me, sugar. Your style is whatever you make it. Here at the start is where you want to set that, and believe me, those long skirts and buttoned-up shirts you wear are not going to win you any points with the audiences. You've got a way about you that could have 'em buying tickets by the thousands.'' He walked around her, sizing her up. "Show a little flash—the hair works, and you've got a great body. God gave you that body. Show it off a little."

"That's out of line," Rachel snapped.

"Okay, okay." Todd replied, holding his hands up to ward off her anger. "It's your call, of course. But if you've decided that you're happy playing country fairs and revival meetings, you don't need me. If you want to open for the Wilson Brothers, I expect you to pay attention or I'm outta here. Think it over."

As soon as she heard the door close behind him she snapped off the tape recorder and threw the offending costume across the room. Then she sat at her dressing table and buried her face in her hands.

"I thought my talent would be enough," she whispered. "God, what do I do now?"

There was a soft knock at the door.

"Come in." Rachel checked her face in the mirror and turned to greet her visitor with a bright smile. "Hi, Pearl, what can I do for you?"

"I think the question is what I can maybe do for you, honey."

Rachel smiled at Ezra's wife. "You've been so good to me, Pearl. I don't know how I would have handled this tour without you along. It's…" She felt tears coming. "It's very different than what I expected."

"It's a lot to get used to, but it does get easier," Pearl assured her. She picked up the costume and hung it on the back of the door. "Todd Mayfield is a good manager. Unfortunately, he knows it, if you get my meaning. Over the years he's gotten pretty cocky about himself.''

"He basically told me it was his way or the highway," Rachel replied.

"He does have a point, honey. Even the boys understand the drawing power of a well put-together body and a tight pair of jeans. The sad truth is that you gotta get their attention before you can expect them to really listen to what you want to tell 'em in your music.''

"I want people to hear the music, not be looking at me. I'm just the messenger. It's the music that's important.''

"But if they don't listen to the messenger…" Pearl let the sentence hang there for a minute.

"I cannot wear *that*," Rachel insisted, jerking her head in the direction of the spandex number Todd wanted her to wear. "Next thing you know, he'll be expecting me to show off my belly button.''

"Maybe we can work together and come up with something Todd will accept. Do you want to try?''

Paul arrived at the theater just as Rachel was taking the stage. Pearl had left him a backstage pass and assured him that she would keep his arrival a surprise. He could not help but notice the difference between Rachel's appearance here and the one he had witnessed that first night in Nashville.

The stage was absolutely dark as an announcer's voice boomed her name. A band struck up a rocking introduction that he finally recognized as one of her songs. Colored lights played over the vast stage and settled on the woman who stood at center stage, a headset microphone hooked over her riotous red hair, which fanned out behind her as she moved from one side of the stage to the other.

She was dressed in jeans that fit her perfectly and a peasant-style blouse that shimmered with some kind of beading that caught the light. She was wearing boots with three-inch heels and she was belting out the song in rhythm with the band that backed her. He had to listen intently to the words to realize she was singing about God and His love and not some sexy rock song.

But she was good, playing the audience, flirting with them, going to the very edge of the stage and then backing up. At the end of the song she pumped one fist high in the air and brought it down for a final thundering chord on her guitar, then took deep bows and smiled broadly as the crowd shouted its approval.

"The changes are a start," he heard Todd Mayfield say to Pearl. "Good work, Pearl. We'll turn her into a hot property yet."

"I'm just trying to help her, Todd. She's got a big talent, and you know it. If I were you, I'd trust that and stop trying to make her into something she's not. Let her be the original she is, not some carbon copy of the latest teen queen."

Paul turned his attention to the performance. Rachel was talking, taking the time to catch her breath from that last energetic number. She perched on the edge of a high stool. The lights narrowed to a single spotlight on her. The band was silent. She strummed the guitar, tossed her hair and gave the introduction.

When she started to sing, there were a few rude calls from the audience, quickly shushed by others. By the time she hit the second verse, a pin dropping would have shattered the rapt silence. Paul peered at the audience and saw their faces focused on Rachel, listening to her, nodding in time to the music. A few were even crying. He looked at Rachel and wondered if she could see beyond the lights. He wanted her to know the effect she was having. He wanted her to understand that her ability to write and sing her songs was enough—more than enough. She didn't need any of the trappings Todd Mayfield was trying to lay on her.

The ballad was followed by two more heart-pumping, stage-strutting numbers, a guitar solo and a song designed to involve the audience. She ended with the song she had sung in Nashville but somehow it had been changed from the haunting ballad that had touched his heart to something he hardly recognized with a blues beat and a whining saxophone as backup.

"Thank y'all so very much," Rachel shouted above the applause at the end of the song. "And now, it's my great privilege and pleasure to introduce the duo y'all came to see tonight—Ezra and Jonah Wilson—the Wilson Brothers."

The lights went to black, and Rachel ran to the side of the stage as the opening number for the Wilsons began. She didn't see Paul at first. As soon as she was offstage, the smile disappeared, and in its place he saw a frown and exhaustion as she reached for a towel and a bottle of water. She shuddered and draped the towel over her shoulders like a shawl. Todd Mayfield was at her side instantly.

"You were good, kid. By the time we get to Dallas, you'll be the name everybody's talking about. Trust me. The changes were great, and you carried them off like you were born to perform. Now, go get changed for the finale."

Paul watched as the agent moved on to berate the lighting technician for being a beat late in the opening.

For a moment Rachel stood there in the shadows against the background of the brightly lit stage. She looked small and very much alone even as she was surrounded by people rushing around making sure the lights and sound were perfect for the Wilsons. Paul stepped forward.

"Hi, songbird."

She looked up in disbelief and then she hurled herself across the few feet that separated them and into his arms.

"Paul! How...what...why didn't you tell me you were coming?"

"And lose my one and only chance to be a groupie? Not on your life. Besides, I told you. I mean to collect on that date even if I have to follow you all the way to Texas to do it." He held her and felt how thin she had gotten in just a couple of weeks. He felt something else. She was trembling. "Hey, what's this?"

She laughed it off. "It's nothing, really. I just get a chill after being out there under those lights. I can't believe you're here." She pushed herself away from him, and he could see that she was fighting to regain her composure.

"Did you see my act?" she asked as she wiped the sweat from her neck. "What did you think?"

"You've made some changes."

"Yeah, well, that's show biz. As Todd says, change or get left behind. What did you think?"

"The ballad was really nice," he said. "Can you see the audience or are the lights too bright?"

"I can see them, but sometimes I'm so scared by how many of them are out there that I have to admit, I try not to look."

"I wish you could see their faces when you sing that ballad. You move them to tears."

"Well, that's why the ballad is where it is in the program. It used to be my closer, but Todd says..."

*If I hear Todd's name invoked one more time, I might have to shake her.*

"Todd seems to have had a big influence."

"He knows his business. Pearl has been a big help, as well. I don't know what I would have done without her."

*Come home,* he thought. *Maybe you would have come home where you belong.* He wondered why he would think such a thing when all the while he had been quietly cheering for her success.

"Hey, I have to change for the finale. Come on with me to the dressing room. How is everybody?"

"Maggie sent cookies."

Rachel laughed, and it was almost her normal laugh. "God bless that sister of mine," she said and led the way to her dressing room. "I hope you've got 'em on you. Suddenly I'm famished."

"Now, that's the Rachel Duke I know," Paul said as he followed her through the narrow backstage area to her dressing room.

He waited in the small room while she stepped behind a curtained area and changed. "I like your hair," he said for no other reason than to open the conversation. "It's different."

"Pearl did it. She says that it's important for me to get it off my face a bit so the lights can pick up my features. She also has been a big help with my makeup."

"Sounds like she's taken you under her wing."

"How's Doc?"

"He's great." He wanted to tell her about the night in the kitchen, the night his father had encouraged him to find the funding and pursue his dream. The time didn't seem right.

The place was a madhouse with people popping in and out to bring her notes or let her know the time she had before she needed to be back onstage for the finale. "I thought maybe after the show you might have time to go somewhere for coffee."

"Sure." She emerged from the curtained area wearing white jeans and a fringed jacket left open over a hot pink tube top. She had piled her hair on top of her head in a haphazard manner. "I just can't believe you're here," she said again and smiled. "Oh, I get it. You have this fellow researcher here in Texas that you just had to see, right?"

"I'm crushed that you would think such a thing," Paul teased back, enjoying the repartee that felt like old times.

"Yeah. Sure," she said, and rolled her eyes. "Maggie got you to come here and check up on me, didn't she?" she asked as she touched up her makeup.

He noticed that as quickly as it had disappeared the edginess was back. "I came on my own, Rachel."

She paused in the motion of applying mascara and looked at him through the mirror. "That's really nice," she said softly.

Paul realized that they were both uneasy. Whether it was the place or what had happened to her since joining the tour he couldn't say. Maybe it was a little of both, but there was something plastic about her. The smile came too readily and was overly bright. She was too thin. The clothes were not in keeping with the woman he'd gotten to know. More to the point, the look and attitude did not seem to fit with her music.

"You sure have made some changes," he said and hoped she might take it as a compliment. She had to go back onstage. This was hardly the time to challenge her about what she had done to herself—or allowed Todd Mayfield to do to her—since leaving Smokey Forge.

"Five minutes," the stage manager called from outside the door.

Rachel pulled on one white high-heeled boot and searched frantically for its mate. Paul saw it sticking out from under a chair piled high with clothes and picked it up.

"Here, let me." He knelt and eased the boot onto her foot.

"You're making me feel like Cinderella," she teased, and this time her voice was less brittle and her smile was genuine.

He stood up. "Prince Charming, I'm not." He opened the door and stood aside to let her pass. "I'll watch from the wings."

The final number of the show was a medley of vintage gospel songs, a tribute to some of the groups who had made the music popular through the years. Paul could see that Rachel was perfectly at ease performing with the Wilsons. Part of that was no doubt because the two brothers were comfortable with their own fame and popularity. She was no threat to them. In fact, bringing her back onstage made them look even better. They were generous enough to foster new talent.

It was Todd's attitude that irritated Paul.

"You're watching a star in the making, my friend," the manager said, nudging Paul with his elbow. "If she listens to me I'll have her at the top of the charts and on her first solo road tour by next summer. Bet you didn't realize there was such a sexy body underneath there, did you, Doc?''

Paul entertained the thought of loosening several of the promoter's artificially whitened teeth.

"Look at 'em," Mayfield continued, calling Paul's attention to the audience. "The senior citizens all want to take her home and feed her, the women all want to be her, and the guys just *want* her. She's a triple threat.

"I thought it was her talent for songwriting and singing that was most important," Paul said fighting to keep his temper in check. "I thought that's why you wanted to represent her."

"Not in this market. It helps, of course, but the name of the game these days is sex appeal and how she'll play across audiences. I saw that she had what it took that first night in Nashville—until she passed out, of course. After that I did a little checking to be sure it was nothing serious and then gave her a call. The music—the voice—we can fix all that with enough amps and backup singers. Not everybody who comes to hear her is here for a religious experience—at least not the kind she sings about."

"So, you're planning to take her songs and make them more secular?"

"No need. Put the right beat behind those words and people hear what they want to hear. She can sing about loving God till the cows come home, and two-thirds of those folks out there will think she's singing about her lover. It's a real win-win situation."

The number ended, and Todd put his fingers to his teeth and whistled loud and long. "Way to go, honey," he shouted as Rachel came running to the side of the stage. "Now get back out there for an encore and sell it, sweetie."

Paul watched her trot back onto the stage, watched her face as the applause and cheers rained down on her. Did she know what Todd had in mind for her career? And if she knew, did she agree?

They ended up at an Italian place sharing a pizza. The Wilsons were there, along with several members of the band and crew. Paul was grateful that Todd Mayfield had stayed behind to settle up with the management of the theater and oversee the packing up of the instruments and sound equipment for the move to Dallas the following day.

"You look tired," Paul said lightly. They had taken a small booth away from the others so they could talk.

"It's just a normal letdown following a performance, and also knowing that we're moving again tomorrow." She smiled. "That's the one thing nobody can prepare you for. The constant moving from one place to another, never being anywhere long enough to see much of the town or meet the people other than those few who get backstage passes for the shows."

"You lost some weight."

She took another bite of her pizza. "The shows take a lot of energy. I'm fine."

He heard the edge to her voice and knew that she thought he was reprimanding her.

"I didn't mean anything by it," he said softly. "Just trying to make conversation."

She sighed and looked at him for a long moment. "What's happened? I mean, we always talked so easily, and now it's like...I mean I'm so glad you came, but..."

He nodded. "I know. It's pretty weird. Maybe it's just being out of our element."

She laughed. "I thought you were always out of your element, Dr. Paul."

He smiled. "Maybe we just need some time."

"How long can you stay?"

He saw her eyes fill with hope. *As long as you need me,* he wanted to say. "I have to get back the day after tomorrow. I booked a flight out of Dallas."

"But you'll go to Dallas with us? You'll see the show there?"

"I'll go with you and watch the rehearsal tomorrow night, but I have to get the flight out at nine the next morning."

"Well, half is better than nothing," she said. She sat back and glanced over at the table where the Wilsons were having their supper. "They think you're my boyfriend," she said and gave him a mischievous grin. "Should we really give them something to talk about?"

He smiled at her. "It seems to me that you tried playing that game once before and it backfired on you."

Her laughter was wonderful to hear, and he began to relax. "Touché," she said.

"I've got something I want to tell you."

She leaned forward. "Tell me."

"Dad has encouraged me to go after the funding for the expansion of the clinic and setting up the mobile unit."

She sucked in her breath in surprise. "Oh, Paul, how wonderful. What changed his mind?"

"You played a big part in it. I don't know what you put in that coffee you had with him, but the man went into high gear. The other night he sits me down and tells me he's worked out this deal with a friend at a teaching hospital over in the next county to help with the patients at the clinic. The hospital will rotate residents through the clinic, freeing me up to devote full-time to this."

"For how long?"

"Forever. They seem to think it's a good deal for their residents to experience that kind of setting. Dad seems pretty excited about it. He definitely likes the idea of being a teacher to these kids."

"And what about the program?"

"I have to find the money. Dad's already come up with a place, and we might be able to get the rent on that donated."

She leaned back again and drummed her palms on the table. "Well, isn't this something? You see, I've been kind of working on things from this end."

"I don't understand."

Her eyes sparkled. "Just wait," she said, and her voice was filled with genuine excitement. "Hey, Ezra, could you come over here for a minute?" The lanky singer pushed back from his table and ambled over to their booth.

"Boy, you folks sure did polish off that large pizza all by yourselves," Ezra commented. "Doc, did you ever see such a little bit of a thing eat like this one does?"

Rachel patted the seat beside her. "Ezra, remember me telling you about Paul's idea for a treatment program for kids from the mountains and from refugee camps overseas?"

"Sounds like a dandy idea, Doc," Ezra replied.

"Can we talk about the foundation?" Rachel prodded.

"Our tax guy told us we'd better find a way to start

spending some of our money for good stuff or be prepared to hand big chunks over to the government tax-
man.'' Ezra grinned and took a long swallow of his
soda. "Shoot, I figure they get their fair share. Why
should I give 'em more if I can spend it on something
that counts?''

"Like kids,'' Rachel broke in. "The Wilson family
has a long history of helping needy children, and—''

"Well, now honey, we don't do anything special. But
the Lord has blessed us a hundredfold, and we figure
we ought to give back something. Who better to give
back to than the young-uns who'll be our future?''

Paul was permitting himself to become cautiously excited. He wondered how much money the Wilsons
could have earned singing gospel music.

"Paul is ready to start the program, Ezra—as soon
as he gets the funding.''

Ezra laughed. "Subtle, ain't she? How much do you
figure on needing, son?''

"That's hard to say at this point. I mean, I've just
begun to—''

"Do you figure two fifty would get you on your
way?'' Ezra asked.

He tried not to be disappointed. Every little bit would
help—even two hundred and fifty dollars. "That's very
kind of you, Ezra.''

Ezra turned so that he was facing the table where the
rest of the family was gathered. "Pearlie Mae, bring
that bankbook I gave you to hold over here.''

Pearl picked up her purse and came to the table.
"Ezra, you know you complain about how much junk
I carry around in this thing, but if you would just get
yourself a safe deposit box somewhere or...'' She rum-
maged through the large bag. "Here.''

Ezra thumbed through the book. "Here it is. Get your phone out, Pearlie."

"They're not gonna be open now," she protested.

"Says twenty-four hours," Ezra replied. "Let's take 'em at their word."

Pearl handed him the cell phone, and he started punching in the toll-free number.

"Mr. Wilson," Paul protested, "this can wait. You can mail me the check."

Ezra held up a finger for silence. "Well, hi there, Amy. They got you working the graveyard shift, do they?" The singer chuckled, then continued. "This here is Ezra Wilson and the account number is eight one seven two six four nine zero. Then there's a dash and the number one eight four seven. Got that?"

"What a country," Pearl said in a stage whisper. "You can do your business twenty-four hours a day, seven days a week." She shook her head in wonder.

"That's it, Amy. Now here's what I need you to do, darlin'. Take two hundred fifty thousand and deposit it to the First National Bank of Smokey Forge, account of Doc McCoy—they'll know him there. Smokey Forge is just a wide spot in the road. Oh, you know it?"

Paul's mouth dropped open.

Ezra covered the receiver with his hand. "That'll be okay, won't it, Paul? Depositing to your daddy's account? I figure it'll simplify the paperwork."

Paul nodded.

Rachel leaned across the table. "You thought he was offering two hundred fifty," she whispered, "didn't you?"

Paul could do nothing more than nod as he kept his focus on Ezra.

"And you thought we small-town types were the bumpkins in this crowd." She giggled.

"I understand, Amy, honey. I'll be in Dallas tomorrow. You all got a branch bank there?" He nodded. "Well, then, I'll trust you to make sure they have the paperwork and I'll just drop by on my way into town and sign my John Henry on the dotted line. Will that be okay, then?"

He listened and grinned. "Why, yes, ma'am, I am *that* Ezra Wilson. My brother Jonah's right here. You want to talk to him?" He motioned for Jonah to come over and take the phone. "Say howdy to Amy," he instructed.

The Wilson brothers and Pearl moved away from the booth as Jonah and Ezra continued their conversation with the woman at the bank.

Paul looked at Rachel. "He just transferred a quarter of a million dollars to my dad's account."

Rachel grinned. "Yeah, when they get off the phone you might want to give Doc a call just so he doesn't have a heart attack when the bank calls him tomorrow morning."

"I don't know what to say."

Rachel covered his hand with hers. "Say that you'll stay in Smokey Forge doing the work God put you here to do."

# Chapter Nine

It had been a long time since Paul had allowed himself the freedom of just having fun for a day. The bus trip to Dallas with Rachel and the Wilsons was a nonstop talk, song and eating fest.

Todd Mayfield saw them off the following morning, admonishing the driver to pay attention to the weather since thunderstorms were predicted. He would take a late morning flight to Dallas and meet them at the hotel.

"On our nickel," Paul heard Jonah mutter as they boarded the bus.

Ezra, Jonah and Rachel rehearsed the song she'd been writing for them to use as their finale. It would be introduced for the first time in Dallas. It was a song filled with hope and sung to a toe-tapping, upbeat melody.

> All the children
> Everywhere
> Give them hope and
> Loving care
> Teach them well, and

Hold them near
It's the children's song
The world must hear

Pearl joined in on the chorus as the bus raced down the interstate.

Children's voices
Raised in song
With God's own help
We right all wrong.

Paul saw Rachel watching him as she repeated the chorus alone to the strum of only her guitar. Her eyes locked on his, and he knew that the song was about his plans for building a program to treat children.

With God's own help
We right all wrong.

Ezra and Jonah cheered the last chords and turned to each other to talk about harmonizing on the chorus. Rachel continued to look at Paul, waiting for his reaction.

"You wrote that for the kids?"

"I wrote it for you," she replied with a shy smile. "Ezra here thinks we might be able to release it on a CD and use the royalties to build the clinic."

Paul's eyes widened, and he turned his attention to Ezra and Jonah. "That's awfully generous."

"Aw, Doc, it's for the kids. Besides, the DJs eat this sort of stuff up, so we know it'll get heavy air time. They play our stuff, we get better known and sell more of the other stuff," Ezra explained.

"Yeah, it's a win-win sit-u-a-tion, as ol' Todd likes to say," Jonah added.

Everyone laughed at Jonah's accurate imitation of the manager.

"I just want us to rethink that middle section a little," Ezra said, and Rachel and Jonah gave him their full attention.

"Paul, would you help me serve up some lunch here? I think they're almost done." Pearl nodded toward the trio of singers.

"My pleasure."

He and Pearl worked in easy silence against the background of the stops and starts of the revised music at the other end of the tour bus.

"She's very talented, isn't she, Pearl?" Paul asked as he spread mustard on bread for turkey sandwiches.

"She's a find, that one. Real star potential, and the best part is, she's as sweet as the day is long."

"What do you think of Mayfield? Is he right for her? To take her where she can go?"

Pearl shrugged. "Todd's one of the best. He has the contacts and the respect—those two things can make a huge difference." She glanced at Paul. "I wouldn't worry too much about Rachel, Doc. She may be sweet, but there's toughness to her. She knows what she wants, and she's got a strong faith to guide her. She'll be fine."

Paul smiled and added lettuce and tomato to the sandwiches. "When I knew her as a kid, I just thought of her as this cute kid with a fresh mouth on her."

"And what do you think of her today?"

Paul looked at Rachel, her eyes bright with excitement as she tried a new harmony Jonah had just suggested. "I think that I might be a little out of my league when it comes to Miss Rachel Duke," he said softly.

"Don't sell yourself short, Doc." Pearl loaded the sandwiches onto a platter and set them on the fold-down table. "Hey, music people, me and Doc are famished."

When they arrived at the theater where they would perform for the week in Dallas, Todd Mayfield was there to meet them.

"We've got problems." That was his greeting as they exited the bus into the drizzling rain. "Pearl, take Rachel there and get on over to the radio station for an interview—the driver's got the address. Ezra, the newspaper's entertainment and religion editors are inside waiting. Where the devil have you folks been?"

Paul found himself standing alone next to the suddenly empty bus as everyone scattered. He saw the limo drive off with Pearl and Rachel before he had a chance to say he'd come along. He felt out of his element. All these weeks since he'd come home, she'd been part of his world. Even the times they had spent at the farmhouse, more often than not their conversation had focused on him or medicine. She was always trying to find out more about him, prodding him to reveal little pieces of himself that he normally wouldn't share with anyone.

When had he asked about her—not her music or her teaching—*her*? He had assumed that because he'd grown up with her sisters, he knew her. He had thought he knew how that upbringing would affect someone who had never really left the tiny town. He had thought his relationship with Rachel was one of doctor and patient with a little of the older, wiser, more sophisticated friend thrown in. When had that changed?

He thrust his hands into his coat pockets and walked away from the theater. He needed to think. He needed to put things into perspective. He needed to figure out how and when Rachel Duke had stopped being the cute little Duke kid and become a woman he might well be falling in love with.

Once they arrived in Dallas, it seemed to Rachel that there was no time to be with Paul. First, she was hurried off to the interview. When that was done, there were rehearsals and sound checks and lighting glitches to be corrected. Paul brought in Chinese food for all of them around seven, and then sat patiently in the empty theater while they rehearsed the finale again and again.

"Todd didn't like our arrangement," she said as Paul walked her the short distance to the hotel. She paused only a second before adding, "I really don't think he likes the song at all."

"It's a terrific song," Paul told her, and resisted adding that Todd Mayfield didn't know everything.

"You really like it?"

He'd never seen her like this, so dubious of her talent, so unsure of herself. "Now, you listen to me, Rachel Duke. That is a remarkable song. Ezra and Jonah believe in it or they wouldn't, for one minute, let it be out there with their names on it."

"Well, that's true. But Todd says it's not right for the end of the show. He thinks we need to go out with something bigger."

"What does Ezra think?"

"Todd didn't talk to Ezra yet. He told me he's doing this for me—for my future. He says we need to think about showcasing me and that I should be what people remember as they leave the show."

"And what do you think?"

"I think it's more important that they remember the

words of the song and that they spread God's message. That's why we're up there."

Paul let out a breath it felt as if he'd been holding far too long. "Well, I'm glad to hear you say that."

Rachel grew very quiet. "What is that supposed to mean?" she asked after several seconds, and her tone was filled with challenge. "You don't like Todd, do you?"

"Not a whole lot," Paul admitted.

"Well, he's not there to win popularity contests. He's there to help me get what I want."

"By turning you into something you're not?" Paul would have taken the words back if he could have.

"By turning me into a viable performer—one who can put people in the seats and get them to leave and head straight for the store to buy what they just heard me sing," she replied tersely.

Paul stopped just outside the hotel entrance. It was after midnight, and the street was deserted. He'd started this. Might as well take it all the way. "Are you listening to yourself, Rachel?" he argued.

She crossed her arms and glanced somewhere over his shoulder, refusing to make eye contact.

"You're letting this guy dress you up in three-inch heels and tight jeans and teach you to strut around like some rock star. I thought he was just changing the outside of you, but I'm really scared that he's beginning to work on the inside, as well."

"Meaning?"

"Meaning that Mayfield is turning you into somebody I hardly recognize, and I have to wonder if when you look in the mirror, you recognize yourself."

He saw in her eyes that he had finally hit the core of her emotions. She flinched as if he had struck her, and then her eyes hardened. "It's been a long day. I'm go-ing inside."

"Not yet." He took her by the arm and started to walk down the street with her away from the entrance to the hotel.

"Paul, I'm tired. I'm not up for a walk, okay?"

"Just around the block. I just need ten minutes with you without Todd or any of the others around, okay?"

She sighed heavily but kept walking.

"Rachel, nobody wanted this more for you than I did. I saw that it was something so important to you, and I really hoped…"

"You don't think I've got what it takes to make it," she said flatly.

"I didn't say that. What I think is that this isn't right for you—something about it just doesn't work for you."

"It's one job—next month, I'll be with some other group. God willing, one day *I'll* be the one out front with some other wannabe as *my* opening act."

"Is this really the life you want? Moving from town to town? Hours on a bus, arriving in town late at night and going straight to some hotel room that looks like the last one and the one that will come next week? You're a people person, Rachel, and…"

"I see thousands of people," she protested.

"Yeah. You're up there and they're out there and if you stretch you can touch a few fingertips during the finale. Don't you miss the real contact? The kids? The conversations?"

"We visit hospitals when we have a chance. We…"

"It's not the same."

"The same as what?" she demanded.

He struggled to find words. "Home," he said finally. "It's not the same as home."

To his surprise, she laughed. "You are hardly the one to lecture me about *home,* Paul McCoy."

"Well, then you'd better hold on to your hat, lady, because I'm not done."

"Oh, yes, you are," she replied, and strode away from him toward the entrance of the hotel.

He caught up to her, dogging her long strides. "You've always told me your music was about spreading the faith, about bringing people back to God. How can you do that if you let this guy lure you away from your own faith with the promise of big-time stardom?"

"He isn't doing that. God won't let that happen," she argued.

"Oh, really. Well, you might want to check in with the Big Guy, because I don't think you've talked to Him in some time—not that I've heard, anyway."

"How dare you lecture me about religion? How dare you lecture me about anything when your own life is a shambles, or was the last time I looked."

"Things change," he said with a shrug and then looked at her directly. "People change, Rach. Some for the better and some not."

She didn't say anything, so he pushed his point.

"Look, I know what a jerk I was being when I first got back to Smokey Forge, but I've come to understand that I can make as much of a difference in and around Smokey Forge as I could anywhere else in the world. The difference is that I'm surrounded by people who care about me and believe in me. You can't buy that on the open market, Rachel, and you sure don't have to leave Smokey Forge to find it. You taught me that."

"I am the same person I was when I got on that bus four weeks ago," she said through clenched teeth in a voice that showed no emotion, just determination. "I have a job to do and it's hard and exhausting and I cannot please everyone all the time.''

''All I'm asking you to do is make sure that *you're* happy with what's happening in your life, and the truth is, Rach, you seem pretty miserable.''

They had come full circle and reached the entrance to the hotel. As soon as they were inside the brightly lit and busy lobby, she broke away from him and dashed across the lobby, catching an elevator just as the doors were closing. This time, Paul made no attempt to try to stop her.

Rachel closed her eyes and leaned her head against the smooth paneled wall of the elevator. Tears dampened her lashes, and as the elevator slowed at her floor, she dabbed at the tears with the back of her hand, just in case someone from the band or crew was in the hall.

She hated that she and Paul had argued, hated more that he had come so close to the truth. She didn't want him to think she couldn't handle things herself, but the fact was that Todd Mayfield *had* changed her in ways she didn't like. She had come to terms with it by deciding that it was all right to be one person onstage and somebody else in private, but lately, that person onstage had become who she was offstage, as well, and Paul was right—that was a person she barely recognized.

When she had walked off that stage the night before and seen Paul standing there, she had run to him as if he were a lifeline. It had surprised her how glad she was to see him, how much she had missed him even though she had only been gone a few weeks. Yet she still resisted sharing the details of her experience on the road with him. Why?

''God, he's my best friend. Why couldn't I talk to

him? He did this really incredible thing—coming all this way just to see me, and what do I do?''

She felt none of her usual closeness to God. The room was completely void of any spirituality, but she plunged on.

''I ruin it. That's what I do,'' she continued. ''What's the matter with me?''

She lay back on the bed and stared at the ceiling, waiting for guidance. The phone rang, and she grabbed it, hoping it would be Paul.

''Rachel? Todd. Now listen, kid, I'm not happy with the way this is shaping up—this finale number you wrote. I've got a couple of guys from the band down here in a meeting room just off the lobby. I want you down here so we can work this out tonight.''

The minute he began talking, Rachel had automatically reached for her shoes and checked her hair in the dresser mirror. Something about the lifeless eyes in the face that looked back at her from that mirror made her stop.

''I've already undressed for bed, Todd. I—''

''Then redress and get down here.''

''Not tonight. I'm tired, and I need some rest. We can fix the number at tomorrow's rehearsal.''

''Maybe if you'd spent a little less time with your doctor friend—''

''Todd, I appreciate everything you've done for me and everything you're trying to do,'' Rachel said and meant it. ''But you're pushing me beyond what I can do. I know myself, Todd, and I know I can perform up to your standards, but you've got to trust that a little and back off.''

There was a long pause at the other end of the line. Clearly, Todd Mayfield was not used to being told to back off, no matter how sweetly the message was delivered.

"You're refusing to rehearse, then?"

"No. I'm doing what I need to do to deliver the very best possible performance tomorrow night. It's opening night, Todd. I want to be at my peak—I want my energy at an all-time high."

Again, a pause.

"Be at the theater no later than eight-thirty in the morning, understood?"

"Thanks, Todd."

"And no doctor hovering around, okay?"

"His flight leaves at nine. He'll be on his way to the airport."

"Good," Todd grumbled, and the line went dead.

As soon as she replaced the receiver, Rachel saw the message light blinking. She dialed into the system.

"Songbird, it's me." There was a pause and he cleared his throat. "Look, I was out of line tonight. I don't know where all that stuff came from. I just didn't want you to go to sleep thinking I didn't believe in you, because I do. You are an incredibly talented and gifted person—talented in your music, gifted in the person that you are...the friend that you are. I don't know what I would have done without your humor and your friendship these last months."

He paused as if expecting her to say something.

"Well, that's it. Get some sleep, Rachel. I'll see you before I head for the airport, okay?"

Rachel slowly replaced the receiver and switched off the bedside lamp.

"What if I didn't have Paul in my life?" she said aloud. "Or Maggie? Or Sara or Doc? I've been pushing them all away ever since I left on tour. What's wrong with me, God?''

The only answer she heard was the soft ding of the elevator bell and hotel guests who had partied late giggling and shushing each other as they stumbled past her room.

The following morning, she dressed quickly and hurried down to the lobby. She didn't want to take a chance that she might miss Paul since he had to leave for the airport. Before their argument the night before, they had planned to meet for an early breakfast in the hotel coffee shop, but there was no sign of Paul.

Disappointed, she stopped at the front desk.

"Dr. McCoy checked out," the clerk informed her.

"I see." She started to walk away.

"Ms. Duke? This was left for you earlier. I was going to have it brought to your room, but since you're here…" The clerk handed her a blue vellum envelope.

"Thank you."

Absently she loosened the flap as she strolled toward the elevators.

Songbird,

It seems to me that we could use a little time by ourselves, and even though time is short, I hope you'll follow the directions in this note and join me for breakfast as planned—only in a slightly different locale.

Paul

The note directed her to take the elevator to the top floor of the hotel and then take the stairway just off the elevator to the roof. As she stepped into the bright morning sunlight, she saw a small round iron French café table with two chairs. The setting was bordered by flowering plants and afforded a breathtaking view of the Dallas skyline. Soft music played.

"If I can't get you back to the mountains," Paul said as he wrapped her in a beautiful shawl, "then I'll have to make do with the mountains at hand." He indicated the skyscrapers surrounding them and led her to the table.

"Paul, this is all so…the setting…the shawl…" She hugged the beautiful garment to herself. It was delicately woven of a fine woolen yarn. It was so lightweight and yet it warmed her, and it ended in a long fringe that drifted through her fingers like the rushing water of the millstream.

"It was Mom's. When you came offstage the other night, I thought the contrast of the drafty backstage and the hot lights onstage might give you a chill. When I called Dad about the money deposit from the Wilsons the other night, I asked him to overnight it so I could give it to you as a kind of a good luck gift for tonight."

"But last night you…"

He brushed aside further comment. "Last night I was being overbearing and overprotective. I understand that now. Last night was not about you or your gift, Rachel. It was about me."

He pulled out one of the chairs and waited for her to sit. There was a single long-stemmed rose on her plate. It was the color of the sunrise. She picked it up and savored its rich perfume.

"I picked that color because it matches your hair," he said with a shrug. He lifted silver servers to reveal eggs, croissants and fresh fruit.

"Paul, this is amazing," she squealed as she served herself.

"And *real* coffee," he announced, filling her cup with a flourish. "No green tea on this occasion."

"And what is the occasion?"

Paul sat opposite her and served himself. "The occasion is the morning of your biggest opening night yet, and that, my dear Ms. Duke, is cause enough for celebration." He lifted his coffee cup in a toast. "You are going to be a major star in whatever field you decide to enter. If that's rock or gospel or some combination of the two, you are going to be wonderful."

She felt the color rise to her cheeks. "Thank you, Paul. It means more to me than you can imagine to hear you say that."

He touched his cup to hers and took a swallow. "I just wish I could stay and be in the audience tonight—or maybe you'd rather see Dad there?" He grinned.

"It would be wonderful to see both of you there," she replied.

As they ate, they talked about mundane things—his flight, her rehearsal, the delicious food.

"What changed your mind, Paul?" she asked when the conversation had died and the plates were empty.

"I realized that in some ways I wasn't talking about you at all when I was warning you about people and difficult decisions."

"Who were you talking about?"

"Me."

She laughed. "That's ridiculous. You know exactly what you want."

"But not necessarily where to find it," he said softly. "It's because of you that I've found that. I guess I thought I was doing the same for you."

"But you did something far more important, Paul. I wouldn't be here today, ready to walk out on that stage tonight, if it hadn't been for you."

He smiled and covered her hand with his. "I guess we must be good for each other, huh?" He reached over and turned up the music. "Would you dance with me, Rachel?"

She tied the shawl around her shoulders and stood up. "I would be honored."

As they moved in time to the music, she saw the sun coming up behind the tall buildings and she felt its warmth. Paul tightened his hold on her as he twirled her around and around. They laughed out loud with delight, and she knew that the physical strength he used to keep her from falling as they danced across the rooftop was a symbol of the emotional strength she'd come to depend upon from him.

"Thank you for being my friend," she said softly when the dance ended, but he didn't let her go.

"Sounds like a song title," he teased, but his voice was unsteady, and he still had not released her.

She rested her head on his shoulder and felt his fingers stroking her hair. She wanted to stay there forever. She wanted everything and everyone to disappear except Paul and this magical moment.

"I have to go," he said finally. "Walk me downstairs to the cab?"

She nodded, retrieved the rose from the table and took his hand.

They didn't speak all the way down to the lobby, just held on to each other, their fingers entwined, their shoulders touching.

"Call me after the show," he said as the cabbie put his luggage in the trunk.

"It'll be late," she protested. "The time difference..."

He shushed her with a finger. "Dad and I will wait up. Call, okay?"

She nodded and ducked her head so he wouldn't see the tears. It was ridiculous to cry. He had come all this way, and she would be home in a couple of weeks. It wasn't as if she'd never see him again. But he already seemed so far away. All of the people who counted in her life seemed miles away.

Paul hooked one finger under her chin and raised her face to his. "Break a leg, songbird," he whispered as his lips brushed hers.

The kiss was brief, and yet in that instant she felt her life changing. She suddenly wanted to reach out, cling to him, beg him not to desert her in this hour of her need. Instead, she smiled and did a little buck-and-wing step, ending it with a bow.

As she had expected, he laughed. Then he got into the cab, and suddenly she was standing on the curb by herself. She looked across the street and saw the marquee of the theater. TONIGHT! The WILSON BROTHERS, Featuring Rachel Duke.

How many times had she dreamed of seeing those words, and yet she stood there staring at them as if they were written in a foreign language.

"There you are." Todd Mayfield's voice boomed as he exited the hotel. "Where the devil have you been, girl? I've been calling your room for an hour."

"I had breakfast," she said softly.

"Must've been some breakfast. Never mind, come on, let's get this rehearsal going. We've got a lot of work to do before show time."

He strode across the street, and when Rachel didn't

follow him at once, he stopped and looked back. "You coming or not?"

"Coming," she replied, but she took one last look down the deserted street where Paul's cab had gone.

"Rachel, what's the matter with you?" Todd barked the words impatiently.

She hurried to catch up with Todd. It was nerves and being with Paul, she told herself as she followed Todd down the narrow alley to the stage door.

As soon as the door slammed behind them and she found herself immersed in the sights and sounds of the theater, she smiled. It was another kind of homecoming, that was all. The people and places of Smokey Forge were one piece of her life. This was another. Surely, there was room for both.

She let the shawl slide off her shoulders and tied it around her hips as she strapped on her guitar and mounted the steps that led from the orchestra pit to the stage. Stagehands were preparing to cover the orchestra pit to allow for three additional rows of seating for the performance. The concert was sold out, and whether people were coming to see her or not, she was going to make sure they knew who she was by the time they left.

She half listened to Todd and Ezra debating the staging of the number as she recalled something Paul had said at breakfast. They'd been talking about the rehab center.

"I've got to give it a shot," he'd told her earnestly. "I mean, look at you. It took real courage for you to go after your dream. You had no guarantees and yet you didn't let that stop you for a minute."

"I don't think it's the same thing," Rachel had replied.

"Yes, in a way it is. No guarantees and no regrets.

Just go out there and give it your best shot. Isn't that what you've done?''

She couldn't deny what he was saying. "Yeah, I did.''

"And it worked for you," Paul said, as if that were some assurance it might work for him, as well.

Rachel absently fingered the song she'd written for him as she thought about his wonderful plans—the good he was going to do.

"Thanks, God," she murmured. "Thanks for letting me be a small part of something so wonderful.''

# Chapter Ten

The plane was delayed. Paul could never figure out how bad weather in Denver affected a flight from Dallas to Nashville, but he had long ago decided that debating the point with airline personnel was a waste of time. He was in the airport café when his cell phone rang.

"Doc? It's Ezra Wilson."

Paul's hand tightened on the phone. "What can I do for you, Ezra?"

The man's voice shook at little as he delivered his news. "There's been an accident. Rachel's taken a bad fall."

"Where is she now?"

"We called the emergency squad, and they've taken her on to the hospital. Pearlie, which hospital was that?"

Paul heard Pearl in the background telling Ezra the name and location of the hospital. Immediately, he started walking toward the airport transit area and held up his hand for a cab even as he continued gathering information from Ezra.

"How did this happen?" he asked.

"Well, we was rehearsing the finale—you know, that nice piece she wrote for us all to do together. Todd had this idea that me and Jonah should start it real quiet like down front at the edge of the stage and then Rachel would come strolling down the stairs there in the background and join us."

"Okay," Paul said, willing the man to get to the point.

"Todd wanted her to just sort of appear up there like the angel she is, so she was climbing up from the back there. It's pretty steep, and it was dark. She was carrying her guitar and had tied some kind of shawl thing with long fringe around her waist."

If she had tripped on the shawl, Paul thought.

"Well, she made it to the top and then Todd had all the lights come on all of a sudden like. I don't think she expected that. She kind of took a little step back when the lights hit her, and that's when she fell."

Paul swallowed bile that threatened to choke him. "Are you telling me that she fell down the steps or off the back of the set?"

"Off the back."

Paul remembered the set from his view of it backstage at the previous stop. A fall from there was equivalent to a fall from a second-story window, at least.

"Was she conscious?"

"Yeah, enough to mumble your name again and again. Pearl still had your number from before when you needed the backstage pass, so we thought we ought to call. She's in a lot of pain, Paul."

"Who went with her to the emergency room?"

"Todd followed the ambulance."

Paul saw that the cabbie was turning off the expressway. "I'm almost there," he told Ezra. "I'll call you as soon as I know anything."

"We'll be waiting and praying, Doc," Ezra assured him.

*Better pray I don't do something that puts Todd Mayfield in the emergency room,* Paul thought grimly.

But when he reached the hospital and saw Todd Mayfield in the waiting room, he almost felt sorry for the man. Mayfield looked old and tired, and all of his usual bluster was gone. He'd been crying, but Paul was in no mood to offer comfort.

"Where is she?" he asked.

Mayfield nodded toward a curtained area down the hall. Paul nodded and went to the desk. He presented his credentials and asked the staff person to contact a doctor he knew who worked out of this hospital. Then he strode toward the curtained area.

The emergency team surrounded Rachel, hooking her to monitors, testing, probing, speaking to her in the loud tones medical teams used when the patient was dazed or floating in and out of consciousness.

"Rachel, can you wiggle your toes?" the doctor in charge asked. Paul kept his eyes riveted on her exposed toes.

Nothing.

"Okay, Rachel, we're going to get you ready to go upstairs, okay?"

Rachel moaned.

"I know it hurts. We're giving you something for the pain, Rachel. Just hang in there with us, okay?"

"Paul," she managed to say weakly.

"I'm here," Paul replied, stepping forward and grasping her hand. When the doctor in charge made a move to prevent him, Paul turned his attention to the team. "I'm Dr. Paul McCoy, Ms. Duke's friend and physician. What are you planning to do?"

The emergency room doctor motioned for Paul to follow him into the hall outside the curtained area.

"We need to get X rays before we can be sure," he began.

"You think it's a spinal injury?"

The young man nodded. "Maybe a broken back—too soon to know for sure whether the spinal cord is involved."

Paul's heart was in his throat. If the accident involved the spinal cord, Rachel could be paralyzed for life. Even if it didn't, there could be complications. Either way, she was facing a long and painful journey back to health.

"Are you a family member?" one of the women he'd met at the desk asked. "Because we really need to check on some insurance here."

"No," Paul replied, his eyes holding the gaze of the woman. "What we need to do is find out how badly she's hurt, whether or not she can be moved, who the best physician available is to do any surgery or treatment, and whether or not that beautiful young woman is ever going to walk again," Paul continued calmly. "*Then,* we'll talk all you want about insurance."

The woman looked stunned and glanced at the young doctor, who indicated with a nod that she should back off. "I'll handle this," he said quietly.

Paul relaxed slightly. He understood that professionally the woman was only doing her job, and the young doctor was trying to do his best, as well. "What's our next move?" he asked, turning his attention to the emergency-room physician.

It took most of the rest of the day, but by early evening they had a diagnosis and a plan of action. Rachel's neck was miraculously intact, but she had a dislocated vertebra. That was causing the paralysis in her lower body.

"We'll stabilize things and realign her spine by the insertion of a titanium rod," the surgeon told Paul as they studied the X rays together. "She's facing three or four hours in surgery, not to mention a long convalescence—and that's if she doesn't get pneumonia or some other complication along the way."

"And then?" Paul asked.

The surgeon shrugged. "I can't give you promises. My guess is that if she's willing to do the work, we can get her to the point where she can walk with a walker or maybe even a cane. The good news is that even though she has sustained a spinal cord injury, only the vertebrae are damaged. Since there is no direct damage to the cord itself, there is every likelihood that the paralysis will disappear once the bones are stabilized. Of course, from the look of these films, there will possibly be some level of permanent loss of function in the hips and legs."

*That's not good enough,* Paul wanted to say, and fully appreciated for the first time the impact a doctor's words could have on loved ones who were trying hard to understand what had happened and why.

As he walked down the hall toward Rachel's room, he tried to find the words he would use to deliver the news. He imagined her questions. Could she go back on tour? Would she lose her big chance because she'd need to be away from performing for so long?

He thought about the way she had looked onstage—her long legs striding across the vast space as if she owned it all, her hair flying free behind her, her smile radiant and her eyes twinkling as she caught the eye of a fan and waved. Surely, they could do something to give her that again. Abruptly, Paul changed direction and headed for the waiting room. He wasn't ready to see her yet. She would see too much in his face.

By the time he got there, Ezra and Jonah and the others from the tour had joined Todd to wait. They all pressed forward when they saw Paul walk into the small room.

"You." Paul pointed to Todd. "I need a word."

The manager moved slowly toward Paul as the others stepped back inside the room.

"How is she, Doc?" The man's voice shook, and his eyes brimmed with fresh tears.

"She's strong and a fighter, which is a good thing since she's facing the fight of her life at the moment."

"Can I see her?"

"In time, and here's what you're going to tell her when you do see her. You're going to tell her that as soon as she's well enough, you'll be booking her for tours and engagements all over the country. She'll open for the best, and eventually they'll open for her. In the meantime, you want her to focus on her songwriting because you are going to set up a recording contract and get play time for her songs on every radio station in the country, understood?"

Todd nodded vigorously throughout Paul's instructions.

"And here's the kicker, Mayfield," Paul added. "You're going to mean every word of it. You're going to deliver and you're going to do it on the premise that Rachel Duke is a gospel singer—not a rock star. Do I make myself clear?"

"You blame me for what happened today?" Todd asked, his eyes widening with comprehension.

Paul looked the short stocky man up and down. "From the way this has shaken you up, I'd say it's more like you blame yourself and I'm offering you a way to ease that guilt." He brushed past the man and turned his attention to others, giving them the news and urging them to go forward with the evening's performance.

"Tell us how else we can help," Pearl said. "There must be more we can do."

"The best thing you can do for her right now is play the concert—sing her songs."

"And pray," Jonah added.

Paul stared at him for a long moment. "That, too," he said, and then left the room.

Later, after he had stopped by to see Rachel and reassure her that she was in good hands with Dr. Hogan, Paul called his father. Earlier they had spoken just long enough for Paul to alert Doc to what was happening and get his advice. Doc in turn had delivered the news to Maggie and Sara. Rachel's sisters were determined to catch the next flight to Dallas, and nothing Doc could say would stop them from doing so. Paul could tell that Doc wanted to come, as well.

"Somebody needs to stay there and hold down the fort," Paul said. "I'll call you the minute she's out of surgery."

Paul's colleague organized the best available surgical team, and the surgery was scheduled for the following morning. If all went well, they would be able to move Rachel to a hospital nearer to Smokey Forge in a few weeks.

"How's she holding up?" Doc asked when Paul called to update him on the plans.

"She's the same as always."

"Well, she's had quite a terrible shock, and it's not unusual for a patient to try to make everything as normal as possible," Doc replied.

"Maybe," Paul agreed, but he knew the emotional wounds had to run deep. What concerned him most was her unwillingness to talk about the accident. The nurses raved about her upbeat attitude and high tolerance for pain. Paul worried that she was pushing the physical and emotional pain inside. In his opinion, she needed to talk about it. She had to be frightened—as scared as he was, Rachel had to be terrified.

That evening he stopped by her room. She was dressed in a hospital gown that seemed way too large for her. Her hair had been pulled into a clip at the nape of her neck, but tendrils of it framed her face. Her skin was very white. Her eyes were shut.

"Rachel?" He called her name softly as he pulled a chair close to the bed.

Her eyes fluttered and opened. She gave him a quizzical smile and looked at him for a long moment as if trying to understand why he would be here at her bedside. He saw realization dawn for an instant, and then the mask was drawn.

"Did Dr. Hogan come by to explain what he plans to do tomorrow?"

She nodded.

"He's the best, Rach."

She smiled. "You doctors say that to all the patients," she said, and her voice was weak as if she was too tired to make more of an effort.

He moved the chair closer to the bed so she wouldn't have to strain to talk. "Well, we have to protect each other, you know."

"I'd rather go into this thing knowing you were holding that scalpel," she said.

"I'm not a surgeon, Rachel, but I'll be right there, okay?"

Again, the single nod. She closed her eyes.

"Maggie and Sara are on their way," he told her.

"Oh, they shouldn't," she said, her eyes open instantly and filled with concern. "The airfare on the spur of the moment must be so expensive, and who'll manage the school?"

"Rachel," he said sharply, and got the response he wanted. Her eyes were riveted on his face. "We need you to concentrate on *you*. We need you to fight, okay?" he said more gently. "I know it's the hardest thing you've ever had to do. But it's vital that you focus only on the surgery and getting well. You can't spend your time worrying about the rest of us, understand? We'll be fine as long as you are. Think about yourself, all right?"

She was quiet for a long moment. Her lips moved, but no words came. She tossed her head impatiently as if rejecting several comments.

"I'm so scared," she whispered, and finally the tears he'd been waiting for, hoping for, came. They rolled down her cheeks, dampening her hair and the pillow, but she made no move to stem them. Instead she reached over and gently smoothed the lines of worry that creased his forehead. "You, too?" she asked.

Paul nodded, trying hard to suppress the emotion that threatened to overwhelm him. He couldn't let her see how frightened he was for her. That was totally unprofessional, and certainly the last thing she needed at the moment. How many times had he sighed in exasperation at family members who succumbed to their own emotions at the very moment when the patient needed their strength and reassurance the most?

"It's going to be fine, Paul," she said. "It'll all work out one way or another. We just have to get used to whatever comes. In time…"

He knew she was talking about God and the fact that in her view, He was in charge. Well, if He was in charge, where the devil had He been when she went tumbling off the back of that set? His anger at a God who would permit such chaos in the life of one as devoted as Rachel stopped his tears.

Not wanting her to see his anger at the God she clearly still needed to see her through this ordeal, he got up and went to the sink. He rinsed a washcloth in cold water and returned to gently wash away her tears. "I'd better go and let you get some rest," he said when the task was done. "You have a big day tomorrow."

"We have a big day," she said softly, and grasped his hand. "Could you get me my shawl? I think the nurses put my stuff in a bag in the closet there." She nodded toward the closet.

He retrieved the shawl he'd given her and covered her with it. "It smells like cedar," he said nervously as he straightened the edges, "because Mom always kept it in her cedar chest."

"It smells like home," Rachel replied softly, and pulled it closer to her face, fingering the fringe as she closed her eyes.

"Sleep well, songbird," Paul whispered, and bent to kiss her temple. He stood there a minute longer, watching her even breathing, knowing she was asleep.

Rachel had no idea what time it was when she woke. The room was very dark although a light shone from

172 The Doctor's Miracle

the hallway. Her heart was pounding, and she suddenly felt as if she couldn't breathe. She tried to get up, and then everything came crashing back.

Her legs didn't work, couldn't work because she was totally immobilized. The large wall clock showed just past three. Later this morning, they would operate. The doctors all assured her that because she was young and in excellent health, they expected things to go well, but she had noticed that they all stopped short of promising that she would walk on her own—much less appear onstage again. Even Paul stopped short of that.

She willed herself to take deep breaths and suddenly realized that what she was feeling was absolute terror. She had never felt more frightened, and for the first time in her life could find no inner strength to stem this panic. That frightened her even more.

"God, I'm so scared," she whispered into the darkness, grateful that at least the hospital rooms were all single-patient rooms. "I can't seem to understand any of this. Thank You for sending Paul back into my life again and again. I have come to rely on him so."

It was the worst sort of lie—she was lying to herself and to God. What she felt for Paul went well beyond relying on him as a doctor and friend.

"Okay, I love him," she whispered. "I know that probably wasn't part of the plan, but it's true, and I don't know what to do about it. Especially now. Oh, why has this happened? Why now?" She would not permit herself to wallow in self-pity and ask, "Why me?"

It was petty and selfish and it implied that her accident should have happened to someone other than herself. She refused to acknowledge that the shadowy concept of *why me* even floated through her thoughts in spite of her efforts to keep it at bay.

She waited. She stared at her lifeless legs. If only she had listened to Paul that night outside the hotel. If only she had admitted the truth of what he was saying to her and gone home with him. But her pride had stood in the way. Her stubborn determination to prove that she could make it on her own in a world bigger than the one her sisters had created for her had taken precedence over everything.

What if God had spoken through Paul and she had refused to listen? If she had gone home with Paul, perhaps they might have worked together on the clinic for the children. Perhaps in time he might have come to care for her as more than a friend.

"Perhaps," she said softly, but would not permit herself to imagine him loving her back. It was too late for that now. Even if there were some miracle that would make him love her, it would be tainted with the suspicion that in part his love grew out of pity, and she couldn't stand that. "Show me what You want me to do, God. I'm so confused and afraid."

She waited for the feelings that had always come to her in such times. The questions that would spring to mind and force her to think through her options and reach decisions. She wasn't necessarily expecting a sign, but there should be something. There had always been *something*.

She closed her eyes, and in the blackness the story of Jesus's anguished night in Gethsemane came to her. He had felt abandoned and alone. He had wondered why it was necessary to go to such extremes. She had no thought, of course, that her own outcome would be remotely similar to that of Jesus, but she suddenly understood that He must have suffered in a way she had never appreciated before. He must have been even more lonely and frightened than she was. Somehow He had found the courage to face what lay ahead. Somehow she must find her own courage and strength and do the same.

The longest night of her life passed, interrupted periodically by the arrival of the night nurse to take her vital signs. The longer she lay there waiting for morning, the more aware of her immobility she became. If she slept, her dreams were disturbing fantasies of life as an invalid, a cripple, her sisters waiting on her, the townspeople pitying her—day in and day out. She tried hard to summon the remnants of what Doc liked to call her spunk, and failed. All she felt was tired and scared. Every waking moment was a silent prayer. "Please, take this burden from me. Please...I don't think I can do this. Please...I'm not strong enough. Please."

They were preparing her for surgery when Maggie and Sara bustled into the room.

"We're her sisters," Maggie told the aide. "Hi, honey, we just saw Paul, and everything's going to be fine."

"Just fine," Sara chorused, and Rachel noticed how her middle sister stayed near the door as if she might at any moment need to make a quick escape.

"You didn't have to do this," Rachel said. "Come all the way down here. It must have cost a fortune."

Maggie's eyes widened. "Are you nuts? Of course, we had to come. Where else would we be?"

"What about the school?"

"The school can manage," Sara replied, and glanced

at the wall clock. "They said they would take you up at eight. It's five after."

"That clock's not right," Rachel said. "Trust me, at three o'clock this morning, it was slow. Now it's fast. Go figure." She smiled to let them know she was kidding.

Maggie brightened immediately. "Well, it's good to see that you haven't lost that dry wit," she said with obvious relief.

*No, just any feeling from the waist down,* Rachel thought, but willed herself to maintain good spirits for the sake of her sisters. "You two look like you haven't slept."

"We had to take a red-eye, and of course, that meant we had to get up at three to dress and get to the airport," Sara replied, clearly glad to be able to discuss logistics.

"You could have skipped washing your hair and putting on makeup," Maggie reminded her. "I got in a whole extra hour of sleep that way." She winked at Rachel.

*So, we're all doing the same thing for each other, for ourselves,* Rachel thought. *Thank You, God, for bringing them here.* She squeezed Maggie's hand. "I'm glad you're here—both of you," she said louder, for the benefit of Sara, still stationed by the door.

"I see Paul," Sara said unsteadily and left the room.

"She's pretty emotional about this," Maggie reported. "Not that I'm not, mind you, but Sara is just plain scared."

"Tell me about it," Rachel replied with a wry smile.

"Oh, honey, what a stupid thing for me to say. I'm just chattering. Sara handles it by running away. I do it by saying stupid things." Throughout all of this she continued to stroke the back of Rachel's hand. "Paul says it's going to be fine," she added almost to herself.

"They all say that, Maggie, and we both know that whatever comes will come. If I'm meant to get better or if I'm not—that's not in our hands or the surgeon's."

"Here's Paul," Sara announced, sounding as if she were introducing a television talk show host.

"Hi, songbird. Ready to take a ride?"

Paul was accompanied by two aides who unlocked her bed and began the process of moving it into the hall and through the corridors to the operating room. Maggie and Sara hovered outside the room, then tried to keep up.

"We'll be right here," Maggie called when they gave up the chase. "Paul?"

"I'll let you know as soon as I know anything," he replied, and his face was set and tense as he kept pace with the rolling bed. He kept one hand on the side of the bed as if wanting to make sure it didn't get ahead of him.

Rachel reached over and clasped his fingers, which made him look at her in surprise. She was feeling groggy from the medicine they had already started through the intravenous drip into her arm. "It's going to be okay," she said and knew her words were slurring. "Really..."

The next thing she realized, she was struggling to come awake. It felt as if she were trying to come out from under a hundred heavy blankets. People were talking, and she picked up snippets of their conversation. Some of it was even directed at her.

"Rachel?"

A woman. Maybe a nurse.

"It's over, and you're in recovery."

"Rachel?"

A man.

"I'm just going to put this oxygen mask on you for a bit."

*Don't!* She was fighting hard to emerge from the blackness that seemed determined to pull her back. She didn't want anything more covering her, holding her down.

She heard the tearing sounds of Velcro and felt people doing things to her lower body, but she still couldn't feel her legs. In fact, she felt numb and weighted down all over.

"Rachel?"

The woman again.

"We're just putting these circulation pads on your legs, okay? You might feel them puffing up now and then, but that's to prevent blood clots, okay?"

*Does it really matter whether it's okay with me or not?*

"Rachel?"

A man's voice. Familiar. Concerned. *Paul.*

She struggled to open her eyes.

"It took a little longer than we planned, but it's over and it went well."

He was holding her hand, and she felt it slipping from his grasp. With a fierce effort she held on.

"I have to go tell the others," he said gently. "I'll see you back in your room. Dr. Hogan's here."

She felt herself falling back into oblivion, felt Paul's fingers sliding away again, and the panic she had felt the night before returned and brought her back to consciousness.

"Paul?"

"Right here." He took her hand again.

"Why don't I go talk to the family," she heard Dr. Hogan say. "I'll see you when you're more awake, Rachel," he added.

"Thank you," she croaked, and her mouth felt like cotton.

"Rachel, it's okay to sleep. You need to rest. I'm right here. I'm not going anywhere." Paul smoothed her hair from her face.

"Set that to music, Doc, and you might have a hit song," she said and smiled.

She had called him Doc, and yet he knew she hadn't mistaken him for his father. Maybe it meant that she was placing the same trust in him that she and dozens of others had placed in his father for years. If so, it felt good. It felt like something he could get used to—especially where Rachel was concerned.

# Chapter Eleven

"Dad, I'm bringing Rachel home," Paul told Doc one night as they sat across the table from each other sharing a late supper. "It's been six weeks—she's not getting any better." His voice faltered as emotion overwhelmed him, and he bowed his head to keep it from his father.

Doc stood and put a comforting hand on Paul's shoulder. "The staph infection set her back quite a bit, son. You know that. It'll just take more time than you planned."

To say that Rachel's recovery had not gone as well as expected was an understatement. Following the euphoria they all shared at the apparent success of the operation, Rachel had developed an infection, requiring more surgery. Her surgeon had insisted on a four- to six-week recovery period with no physical therapy until he could be sure that she was completely out of the woods in terms of more infection or possible pneumonia.

The longer-than-anticipated recovery had left her

weak and postponed the start of therapy to rebuild her muscles and strengthen her back. The truth of the matter was that the long recovery from the infection had caused her muscles to atrophy and set her even further back following the surgery. Paul had alternated between spending long weekends in Dallas and flying to Tennessee to work on setting up the mobile unit and expansion of the clinic during the week.

Frustrated with the lack of any real progress from one visit to the next, Paul decided Rachel might do better if she came home. He had sent Jan Stokes, the chief therapist he had hired to develop the program for the rehab center in Smokey Forge, down to Dallas to assess the situation with him.

"A lot of surgeons have doubts about the value of therapy in postsurgical patients," Jan told him. "The research that would prove efficacy is pretty sketchy, so it's not unusual that a surgeon would take a wait-and-see attitude."

"Can we move her safely?"

"That's up to the surgeons and the team there to decide."

"But would you move her?"

"Ordinarily, no, but given the circumstances…"

Paul had confided in Jan his concern that Rachel was becoming more emotionally fragile with each passing week. Her stubborn determination to maintain a positive outlook in the face of setback after setback worried Paul. He had only seen that eternally cheerful facade crack once.

It was the Wilsons who had seen to it that Rachel's entire family and Doc were flown to Dallas for the Christmas holiday when it became clear that Rachel would not be home as planned.

Ezra and Jonah had brought a huge fresh-cut long-needled pine tree to the hospital's private dining room for doctors—a space they had persuaded Dr. Hogan to let them take over for the evening. Pearl had provided the decorations as well as the food. Several members of the staff and other patients from Rachel's wing had been invited to the special trim-the-tree and caroling party— a party that would feature the famous Wilson Brothers to lead the carols and Doc as Santa Claus.

They had all worked together in secret to prepare the surprise for Rachel. When her nurse had wheeled her into the room on the pretense of meeting with Dr. Hogan before he took off for a couple of days, everyone had serenaded her with "We Wish You a Merry Christmas."

Only Paul had been concerned when Rachel started to cry. The others all found it a natural reaction to the surprise and the kind generosity of the Wilsons. Paul saw that beneath the polite smile and the tears, Rachel was not at all herself. Rachel was upset. He watched as she called upon some inner strength and threw herself into the festivities, but he saw that her eyes were dull and her smile was locked in place by two tense lines at the corners of her mouth. He knew at once that they had made a huge mistake in doing this.

She almost pulled it off until Ezra picked up her guitar and invited her to sing along with them the song she had written for their holiday concert tour. Rachel had stared at the guitar as if she'd never laid eyes on it before. At last, she took it, and Paul saw that the smile trembled unsteadily. She strummed her fingers across the strings, but the instrument was too heavy for her to support, and her efforts were awkward and clumsy.

*Let it comfort her,* Paul thought, unaware of the

prayer he'd just conjured. *Let this be the instrument of her healing.*

To everyone's dismay, she burst into tears, thrust the guitar toward the nearest person, who happened to be Maggie, and rapidly wheeled herself toward the exit.

"I'll go," Paul had said quietly as the others looked on in stunned silence.

"It's just too much for her right now," he heard Maggie say as he hurried to catch up with Rachel.

She had cleared the automatic doors, which had swung shut behind her, leaving her alone in the empty hallway. When Paul came through the doors seconds later, he saw her shoulders heaving with sobs.

"It's okay," he said as he knelt next to her chair. "Everyone understands." He put his hand out to touch her, and she brushed it away.

"It's not okay, Paul," she replied angrily. "And *I* don't understand. I don't understand at all." She rolled herself a few feet farther down the hall, then stopped and sat there pounding the armrests of the chair with the flat of her palms. "I can't do this," she said, more to herself than him.

"You can," Paul assured her. "You're strong and you have more courage than anyone I know."

She answered that statement with a mirthless laugh that clearly indicated her disbelief, and refused to look at him.

"Hey, listen to me. We're going to get through this. We're all here and we're all going to do everything we can to..."

She looked at him for the first time since leaving the room. Her face was wet with tears, and her eyes reflected the anguish of her deepest self. "That's just it. I have dragged all of you into this with me. What are you all doing here? What about the fact that Maggie and Sara and the twins have spent a fortune coming down here yet again? What about the fact that because of me Doc has shut down the clinic? What about the fact that the Wilsons are spending their precious holidays here with me instead of back home with their own family where they belong?''

"You're blaming yourself for what people want to do for you?" Paul was astounded. Then he understood for the first time. "You're blaming yourself for the accident," he stated flatly.

She jerked away from his touch. "I don't know who to blame," she shouted. "I just know this thing has happened to all those people in there as well as to me, and they don't deserve it."

"And you do?"

She stared at him and then turned away. "I don't want to talk about this."

"I do. Something has happened. Tell me what it is."

She looked at her hands for a very long time. "The doctors here are pretty sure I won't make a full recovery—I won't walk on my own again," she said softly.

Paul swallowed. Dr. Hogan and the others had told him the same thing. He had asked them to let him tell Rachel. "They told you that today?"

"Earlier this week." She gave another mirthless laugh. "It was my own fault. I just kept going on and on about the timeline I was developing for getting well, and poor Dr. Hogan got this expression on his face. You know, I think he's come to like me—to be okay with my kidding around with him. At first, he was so serious."

*Of course, he likes you. The man is probably half in*

*love with you. Who wouldn't be? You make everyone you meet feel as if they can move mountains.*

"So he told you."

"He said he couldn't let me go on living on false hope. He said I was strong enough to face the truth and build a timeline on that."

The door behind them opened a little, letting the muted sounds of the party escape into the hall. "You two okay?" Pearl asked.

"Yeah," Paul replied. "We'll be right in."

"I can't go back in there," Rachel told him. "I hurt their feelings."

"Then go back in there and let them do what *they* need to do for you."

"Put on an act?"

"You were doing a good job of it when you first entered the room," he challenged her.

"I can't play or sing. I can't."

"I don't think that'll come up again tonight."

He saw her struggle with her natural tendency to do what was best for the people in the room behind her and what was obviously her wish to just be alone.

"Okay, if I go back inside, then after this, I want you to make up something that says they need to stay away. I can't worry about them neglecting their own lives to hover over me."

He nodded. "Fair enough. No visitors for the month of January. How's that?"

"That means you, as well. You need to focus on getting the center going, and this business of being there during the week and running down here every weekend has to stop."

"No deal," he said flatly and folded his arms defiantly across his chest. "I'm not going to stop coming here, Rachel."

She frowned and then smiled. "All right, we'll compromise. Keep them home and you can come on the weekends. Do we have a deal?"

"We have a deal."

She sat very still for a long moment, then turned her chair so that she was facing the door to the dining room. "Okay," she said under her breath as if preparing herself for a race or Olympic event. She pushed herself toward the door.

He held the door for her and watched her enter the room. She smiled shyly and asked everyone to forgive her outburst. He saw the relief in their faces and knew that she had reassured them.

"What's wrong with this picture?" he mumbled to himself as Rachel accepted a gift from Pearl and made a great fuss over the wrapping. *She's taking care of everyone but herself,* he realized, and knew that agreeing to her terms was indeed the best way to get her to concentrate on herself instead of the others.

So he had gone every weekend and watched her fight for every minute improvement. It had been six long weeks, and enough was enough. This weekend he would not come home without her.

Rachel leaned close to the window and watched as the plane circled the mountains—*her* mountains. Somewhere down there was Smokey Forge. Somewhere down there was home.

In the weeks since they'd made their deal for him to keep everyone away and stay away himself, she thought she had made real progress. Emotional progress—the physical side of things would come in time. She felt prepared to see her family again, to be with them and reestablish old routines.

She glanced over at Paul, his attention focused on putting away his laptop. For now, she was pretty sure she could actually be in the same room with Paul without fantasizing about what life might be like if he loved her. In the weekends they had spent together in Dallas at the hospital, she had worked hard at keeping things light between them. She thought she had convinced herself that being his friend was just as good as being the woman he would eventually love and build a future with.

Yet with each mile that brought them closer to landing, she knew that she was only fooling herself. She loved him, and maintaining a relationship based on simple friendship would be harder than learning to walk again.

"If you don't mind waiting until the others have deplaned," the attendant said as the crew prepared the cabin for landing, "I'll have a skycap assist you into your wheelchair."

Just like that, reality came crashing back. For a little while, she had felt normal again. Now, she had to face the truth and the future that came with it.

She used a wheelchair. She *needed* the wheelchair. In time she would become stronger and less dependent on the chair, graduating to a walker and perhaps—if things went really well—to a cane. The doctors had made it clear that such progress was not entirely out of the realm of possibility. Walking independently again, however, definitely was not an option in their minds. The aftereffects of the infection had been too severe.

She understood that she was fortunate. The doctors had told her that by all rights she should never have been able to walk at all. They were frankly amazed at her strength and determination. After meeting with Jan Stokes, they had also agreed that the program Paul was setting up for the children in Smokey Forge offered her the best equipment and professional help to achieve her goal.

"You okay?" Paul asked as the other passengers filed past them.

"Sure. It's good to be home." She laughed. "Frankly, it's good to be anywhere outside that hospital."

"I'll get your chair." He followed the last passenger off the plane, and Rachel collected her things. "God," she said softly as she bent to retrieve her bag from under the seat in front of her. "Even though I can't seem to feel You as close as usual, I know You are out there, and I need Your help more than ever. Please help me make this easier for them and give me the strength I'm going to need to get through the days and weeks to come."

"Ready, ma'am?"

The skycap and one of the airline attendants assisted her the short distance from her seat to the door of the plane. Each step was like running the hundred-yard dash. The pain was excruciating, and she had to concentrate so hard to make her legs do so little.

"Your chariot, Miss Duke."

Rachel looked up and saw Paul waiting with the wheelchair just outside the door to the plane.

"Thank you, kind sir," she replied as they all helped her into the chair.

"Your sisters await," he whispered as he pushed the chair up the jetway. "I'm afraid they insisted on coming." She knew he was teasing. There had never been a doubt that Maggie and Sara would be there.

"Just the two of them? Shucks, and I thought there would be a brass band at a minimum," she teased back.

As soon as they cleared the door and entered the terminal, Maggie and Sara rushed toward her. Rachel held out her arms to receive their hugs, and in that moment she knew that there were indeed many reasons it was good to be home at last.

"Look at you," Maggie said, bubbling excitedly. "You look fabulous. I like your hair that way."

Rachel touched her hair self-consciously. "One of the aides talked me into cutting it some and letting it be straight."

"Well, hallelujah," Sara added with a smile. "Ever since you were a kid, you've had this silky-straight hair and you kept trying to curl it. This is much better. It's you," she announced. "Paul, what do you think?"

"I think she could shave her head and she'd still be beautiful," he replied. "Can we go now or were you ladies planning on setting up housekeeping here in the airport?"

"The kids at school can't wait to see you," Maggie told Rachel as they all moved toward the exit. "They've planned a special assembly in your honor."

"I was thinking..." Rachel began.

"And wait till you see Paul's traveling clinic," Sara interrupted. "It is truly like a hospital on wheels."

Rachel looked over her shoulder at Paul, who was grinning with pleasure. When they were together on the weekends, he had shown her sketches and plans for the van and expansion of the clinic, getting her ideas, wanting her to be part of what she had inspired him to create. "I can't wait to see it all for myself," she said.

"You won't have to wait for long," Sara replied. "We drove it here today so you could see it first thing, and later—if you're up to it—we'll take a tour of the center."

"You are not going to believe the changes in the old hospital building," Maggie added. "Oh, honey, it's just so good to have you home."

The ride home flew by as her sisters talked over the top of each other, filling her in on the gossip and the happenings in Smokey Forge since she left. She relaxed and enjoyed it all. Family and friends—that was blessing enough for anyone, she thought as she listened to Maggie and Sara laughing at their own stories. She could rebuild her life. She could live with any residual disability, because other than her physical condition everything else was the same.

Paul drove through town, past the clinic and on to the building that would house the center for the children. "We'll just drive by for now," he said. "Later I'll give you the full tour."

"It's amazing—just from the outside," Rachel said as he slowly drove around the perimeter of the building. "You've added that deck area—and oh, look at how it's all been opened up with the skylights."

"Your idea," he reminded her.

"But to actually see them…" She craned her neck to get a good view as he drove slowly past the clinic.

"When it's done we'll have a dedication, and the Wilsons have promised to come," Maggie told her. "Of course, there's lots of money to be raised before we can really get things going."

Rachel saw Paul cast Maggie a look in the rearview mirror, and Maggie suddenly was quiet.

"We're going to put up a plaque in honor of the Wilsons," Sara added, filling the gap.

"It's wonderful." Rachel sat back as Paul turned a corner and they started up the hill that led to the house. Rachel felt a twinge of nervousness as she turned her attention to the realities of being home again. The bedrooms of the house were all upstairs—her room was upstairs. Through all the trials and good times of her life, her room had been her refuge. How many hours had she spent lying on her stomach, staring out the window and planning her future? Now she supposed they had set up some makeshift arrangement downstairs, at least for now. She prepared herself.

"We've made a few changes at the house, as well," Paul said quietly as if reading her thoughts.

The first change was a temporary ramp off the gravel driveway that she could navigate to the porch. The second was a chairlift on the stairway inside.

"We thought you'd be most comfortable in your own room," Maggie told her. "It was Doc's idea."

"You went to so much trouble," Rachel replied, fingering the controls of the lift.

"Insurance can be a wonderful thing," Sara said as she began bustling around organizing the luggage Paul had unloaded from the van. "And it's a wonderful contraption for getting these suitcases upstairs," she added as she piled them onto the seat of the chair and pushed the button to send it up.

"Let's have something to drink," Maggie suggested and headed for the kitchen.

Rachel wheeled herself slowly through the house toward the kitchen. It all looked the same and yet different, and she realized that the difference was her vantage point. She was seeing everything from the perspective of the wheelchair.

"You okay?" Paul asked, coming alongside her. "Maybe you should rest. It's been quite a full day already."

He looked worried and a lot more like a mother hen than a doctor. She smiled at him.

"I'm fine," she assured him. "I've got lots of time to rest. I just want to be home and catch up on everything. Did you get the work finished for the center this week as planned? How close are you to opening?"

"The physical therapy area is done. Jan's been incredible in overseeing that."

"It was Paul's first priority," Maggie added as she served them cold milk and gingerbread. "Can't imagine why."

"It's important that you be able to start your therapy as soon as possible," Sara explained to Rachel, unaware that she was stating the obvious. "Paul didn't want you having to travel to some specialty hospital for that."

"In addition to Jan, we've been able to hire another first-class therapist," Paul told her. "And after they saw the advantage of rotating interns through the clinic to help Dad, the university wants to use the center as a training ground for its physical therapy interns."

"Paul, that's wonderful. When do you start seeing patients for real?"

"First thing tomorrow," Maggie said before Paul could answer. "You're scheduled to be there at eight."

Rachel felt her smile falter. She knew Maggie meant well, but it was still hard to think of herself as a patient. "I'll be there," she said cheerfully and took a sip of her milk to buy some time to get her emotions under control. It was the one facet of her being that she felt she still did have control over and she was determined to make things as easy as possible for the people she loved.

As usual Paul seemed to see right through her. He reached over and covered her hand with his. "I would like you to come down and try out the equipment and the routine," he said. "If it's not right or if you and Jan don't hit it off, we'll make other arrangements, okay?"

"I'm sure everything will be just fine," she said, her sunny smile firmly in place. "And as long as I'm there I might as well put Jan through her paces."

"Heaven help the poor woman," Sara said, and rolled her eyes as they all shared in the laughter.

Paul had been watching her carefully ever since they had arrived at the airport. To all outward appearances, she was the same, but there was an edge to her. It was as if she were always on guard, watching herself, holding her emotions in tight check. He knew that her progress was not what she had hoped to achieve after all this time, even though she didn't say anything. She simply accepted the well-meaning compliments of others about how far she'd come with her usual grace and good humor.

He saw how sensitive she was to the wariness of others and how quick she was to put them at ease with a quip or a smile. That was the way she had always been. Still, something was missing. He studied her closely as Maggie bustled around the kitchen serving them. Sara stood off to one side, observing as usual. Everything was normal—except Rachel. She looked the same, and yet she was different.

He saw her reaction to Maggie's comment about her

being the center's first patient and knew instantly what had changed. Her confidence was gone. That self-assurance that had been her trademark since childhood was absent. That thing he had first noticed about her—that she approached the world as if she had inside knowledge—was nowhere to be found in the person sipping milk and smiling at her sisters.

"I have another surprise for you," he told her later that evening as he sat on the side of her bed. She had finally admitted to being "a little tired" after the long day. Maggie and Sara had helped her get into bed and then insisted that Paul come upstairs to be sure that she was indeed all right.

"Another surprise? I don't think I can take much more. It's been a really full day."

She sounded polite and distant, as if she were talking to a stranger. He wanted to shake her and remind her, *This is me.* He had saved this news because he wanted to tell her when they were alone. He had imagined her face when she heard the news—the way it would light up—and he had selfishly wanted to have that moment for himself.

"Sami's coming here."

In that instant all the wonder he'd come to expect from her for even the most ordinary happenstance of life was reflected in the warm glow of her emerald eyes.

"Oh, Paul, how fabulous," she said as tears brimmed. "But, how?" She grabbed his hands and held them tight. Large tears plopped onto the backs of his hands. Her tears.

"Hey, this is *good* news," he reminded her.

She smiled. "I know. It's just that everything seems so laden with emotion for me these days." She shrugged and sniffed loudly. "I don't know. It all feels so strange—*I* feel strange. I feel like a stranger in my own body."

"It's your first day home, and so much has happened since you left," he reminded her. "I should have saved this news for tomorrow when you were less tired."

"No. Please, tell me about Sami," she urged, settling back into the pillows her sisters had insisted on piling onto the bed. "When do I get to meet him? How did you pull this off after all this time?"

"He arrived in the States three weeks ago, but he's been at Georgetown University having surgery. You two have a lot in common. Sami's going to need a lot of therapy now that he's had the surgery. I'm counting on you to help him through that."

"Who's with him now?"

"For now he's alone. His aunt has taken his two sisters and returned to their village. Sami refused to go back there."

"That's understandable. The memories must be horrible for him," Rachel said softly, then she realized the impact of what Paul had just said. "Do you mean that he's come all this way on his own?"

Paul smiled. "I told you he was resourceful. Somehow he was able to make the arrangements, probably by conning some of the relief workers to help him get where he needed to be."

"But the cost—the money..."

Paul looked away, and she noticed that his cheeks were flushed.

"You paid for this, didn't you?" she asked.

Paul nodded. "It's not nearly enough. I wish I could get them all out of there, but it's a start."

She reached for him, wrapping her arms tightly

around his neck. "You are the dearest man," she whispered.

Having her hug him felt so right—like his own homecoming of sorts. "Well, Sami's first order of business is going to be to meet you," he said as she pulled away. "He's already made me promise that."

She smiled. "I'm looking forward to it." She leaned back against the pillows.

Paul stood. "Boy, some doctor I am. Here you are exhausted, and I'm rattling on and on when what you need most is to get to sleep." He bent and kissed her forehead as he clicked off the bedside lamp. "Welcome home, songbird."

Rachel was glad for the darkness that did not permit him to see how the nickname he had coined for her and that she had treasured suddenly seemed so foreign to the person she had become. After he left the room, she focused on Sami. As Paul had said, he was going to need a lot of support and understanding once he arrived, and that was one thing she could give him—one thing she could do for Paul.

# Chapter Twelve

It was harder than Rachel had imagined keeping up the facade of cheery optimism with her sisters and well-meaning neighbors and friends who flooded her with cards, gifts and visits. Outwardly, she was determined to face the world as one who had faced the reality of her injuries and was getting on with her life in as normal a manner as possible. Inside, she was struggling to stay afloat amid the debris of her emotional and physical malaise.

She was surrounded by people who loved her, cared for her, and yet she had never felt more alone. To her chagrin, sometimes she had to fight to maintain an outward appearance of appreciation and gratitude for all their kindness. It frustrated her that she couldn't think of anything she might do to repay the kindness.

"I can do it," she snapped at Maggie one morning when her eldest sister insisted on helping her dress as if she were a two-year-old.

"I know," Maggie replied. "I just want..." Her voice faltered, and she turned her attention to the bureau where she busied herself replacing a sweater Rachel had rejected.

Rachel realized that she had taken her frustrations out on her sisters more than once in the last several days. She pushed herself off the edge of the bed and, using the furniture as crutches, made her way to Maggie's side. "Don't mind me," she said, hugging Maggie, leaning on her. "I just got up on the wrong side of the bed this morning."

They shared a laugh, for it was true that in rearranging the room so that Rachel would have everything she needed at hand Maggie had moved the bed to the opposite wall.

"We could put it back the way it was," Maggie suggested.

*No, we really can't,* Rachel thought, and knew that she was no longer thinking about the arrangement of the furniture. She hugged Maggie once again. "It's fine. Something different," she assured her. *Like me.*

It was Paul who finally confronted her, and when he did, Rachel realized that the most upsetting thing about the way people had treated her was the way everyone tiptoed around her, afraid of upsetting her, afraid of saying or doing the wrong thing. Paul's anger came as a relief.

"What is your problem?" he asked one night when she had gone up to her room immediately after supper.

"I'm a little tired," she lied, knowing it would be hours before she slept.

"From what?"

His tone surprised her.

"What is that supposed to mean?" She didn't even try to keep the edge from her voice.

He sat in the rocker across from her bed. "It means

that ever since you came home you've been hiding. Worse than that, you've been acting like an invalid. I know the infection and second surgery set you back a lot, but the time has come to get off your duff and work at getting stronger. You've given up.''

''I have not,'' she declared.

''Really? When's the last time you came to the center?''

''Day before yesterday.'' She shot the words back and folded her arms defiantly across her chest.

He leaned back and pushed the rocker into motion with one foot. ''I see. And the reason you weren't there yesterday or today or three days last week was because you just had so much to do?''

''I don't think sarcasm is necessary.''

''I think it is if that's what it takes to get you to snap out it.''

She pounded her legs with her fists. ''I am not going to *snap out* of this…at least not completely. For an active person like me, that takes some adjustment,'' she said angrily. ''And what would you know about it, anyway? The pain. The work that produces no results. What would any of you know about it? You're all whole—the picture of health.''

He pantomimed playing a violin, knowing it would enrage her further. ''Poor baby.''

''I've tried the regimen your therapists have set for me. I know you've given them stuff to have me do based on your own research, your own consultations with your doctor buddies. Well, *you* try doing those exercises over and over. You try gritting your teeth against the pain. You try….''

He stood up and moved toward her. She shrank back against the pillows. ''What have you done with Rachel, lady?'' he growled angrily. ''She was never a quitter. She was never one to let a little thing like adversity get the best of her. She looked at a situation and sized up what she needed to do and then she *did* it. Where is that woman?''

The look she gave him was so forlorn, so utterly without hope that it broke his heart. ''I don't know,'' she whispered, her eyes wide with panic. ''I'm trying to find her, but I feel so—'' she faltered and swallowed hard ''—alone.''

She started to shake all over, and he gathered her into his arms and held her. ''I'm here,'' he said again and again as she clung to him. ''We're going to get through this. I promise you that.''

Later, after she had promised to be at the center the following day and given in to the exhaustion of the outburst, he stood at the door of her room watching her sleep.

''God, where are You?'' he whispered. ''Now in her hour of need, where have You gone? If You really exist, why have You deserted the one person who has always put You first?''

No answers came. He hadn't really expected any.

Determined not to let Paul bear the burden of her physical and emotional rehabilitation, Rachel forced herself to get to the center early the following day. Jan Stokes, the lead therapist, was working with other patients, so Rachel wheeled herself to the hand weights and began some warm-up work.

As she lifted the weights, she watched the faces of the other patients. One was a teenage girl who had been in a car accident. Rachel saw the girl's fear as she tried each exercise. She understood that fear, understood the pain the girl was experiencing. She knew that subconsciously, the girl was thinking, "If it hurts this much, how could it be a good thing?"

She looked up and saw Paul watching her from the entrance to the therapy area. She nodded in greeting and turned her attention to the repetition of the hand weights. Out of the corner of her eye, she saw him cross the room. He paused to speak to Jan and the girl, offering some comment that made the girl laugh. Rachel saw in the girl's eyes that she was a little infatuated with Paul. It was normal.

"Hi." Paul bent next to Rachel's chair, placing himself at eye level with her. He smiled. "I'm glad you're here."

"You didn't give me a lot of options," she replied. Then she smiled at him. "You knew very well that I would be here after you practically accused me of being a coward last night."

He shrugged. "Whatever works. Why don't you try this one?" He handed her a heavier weight. "That one is way too easy for you. You're hardly exerting any effort."

"I thought Jan was the therapist," she reminded him.

"Yeah, but I'm your friend," he said softly. "And as such, I'm going to keep you honest to yourself." He kissed the top of her head as he stood up. "Got to get back to work. See you tonight?"

"Sure."

After Paul left, Rachel had her best session yet with Jan. When she finished, she was exhausted but exhilarated, a sharp contrast to her usual mood. Jan had kept her so entertained with stories of other patients and their excuses for not working at their therapy that she had hardly noticed the time and effort.

"You're making progress," Jan assured her as they sat together sipping orange juice. "They did excellent work with the surgery, and if we can keep building on that, you're going to be amazed at how quickly you are out of that chair for good."

Rachel recognized it for what it was—the halftime pep talk. She knew Jan believed in what she was saying, believed it was part of her job as a therapist to keep her patients thinking positively. The problem was that Rachel still had doubts. No, it was more than that. She had no faith in Jan's prediction. The truth was, she had no faith at all these days.

"I have to go," she said, forcing a smile for Jan's sake.

"See you tomorrow," Jan called after her.

Rachel noticed that it was not a question. She wheeled herself out of the room and down the hall.

"Oh, let me get that door for you, honey." An older woman who had obviously been bringing her grandson for an appointment retraced her steps to open the door for Rachel.

"Thank you."

"Oh, honey, you are entirely welcome."

Rachel saw the pity behind the smile, knew that the woman was probably thinking what a shame it was that she was so young and in that chair.

*I don't need the chair all the time,* she wanted to call out after the woman. *Most of the time, I can manage quite well with my walker, and it's not entirely out of the realm of possibility that one day soon I could actually walk with a cane and not need anything more.*

But the thought gave her little comfort. Walking with a cane was, in her mind, only a tiny step beyond needing the walker. She wanted to walk free again. She wanted to run. She wanted to skip and dance.

"I don't want pity," she whispered to herself, and gripped the arms of her chair as she fought to get her anger and despair under control.

At any other time, her attention would have been on the child. At any other time, she would have been touched by the older woman's concern. At any other time she would have engaged the woman in conversation, oblivious to her own condition as she focused on the woman's obvious worry about her precious grandchild. But she wasn't that person anymore.

"God, You have always been *in* my life, not Somebody I was waiting to meet in the hereafter," she said as she pushed herself determinedly down the hall toward the exit. "Where are You?" She paused to wait for the automatic doors to open. She looked out at the gray winter afternoon. "Where have You gone?" she whispered.

With a heavy sigh she pulled on her winter jacket, noticing in the process that the sweatshirt she had put on with no more thought than that it matched her jeans read, Expect a Miracle.

She let out a cynical bark of a laugh as she zipped the jacket closed over the words that seemed to mock her.

Paul had seen her leaving. His first instinct, as always, had been to go to her. She'd looked so bewildered as she wheeled herself out the automatic doors and down the ramp to where Maggie waited to take her home. Her thin shoulders had hunched with the effort of pushing the chair, or maybe it had been the effort of holding her spirit together. He had to do something.

They were all worried about her—Maggie, Sara, Doc. She was eternally cheerful and upbeat whenever they were all together. Maggie told him that with some rare exceptions, she maintained that facade even when she was alone with one or both of her sisters. Both sisters agreed that they would be far more comfortable with some cracks in that cheery armor.

"What are we to do?" Sara asked later that afternoon when Paul stopped by the school. "She's so stubborn and determined to take the burden off us by stuffing all of her feelings inside. Even Pastor Griffith hasn't been able to penetrate it. Why, when he stopped by the house the other day and prayed with us, I saw Rachel looking out the window."

"As opposed to?" Paul asked.

"Bowing her head, folding her hands, closing her eyes." Sara ticked off the list on her fingertips. "Rachel would never disrespect the Lord," she added.

"So, looking out the window was out of character?"

Sara released an exasperated sigh. "Yes, Paul, completely out of character."

Paul didn't find it particularly strange. He'd certainly been guilty of gazing out the window on many occasions. Then it hit him. He gazed out church windows or let his mind wander whenever the topic of religion was at hand because he had lost his faith years ago. Rachel was always either talking *about* God or, more likely, talking *to* God.

"Has she been to church since she got back home?" he asked Sara.

Sara shook her head sadly. "She always claims to be too tired or not feeling well. It's hard to argue with that, although, if you ask me—"

"Well, this week she's going," Paul interrupted, "even if I have to take her there myself."

On Sunday morning, Rachel was sitting by the living room window sipping a second cup of coffee when she saw Paul coming up the front walk. She blinked and looked again.

It wasn't that it was so odd to have him stop by. These days he seemed to spend every spare minute at the house. The thing was, this morning he was wearing a suit complete with a crisp white shirt and a tie, not to mention dress shoes. She could not remember ever seeing Paul in anything other than running shoes, and she certainly had never seen him wear a suit and tie.

"Maggie?" she called without taking her eyes off Paul. "Paul's here. I think something may have happened to Doc."

Maggie rushed into the room from the kitchen. "Why on earth would you think that?"

"He's wearing a suit and he looks serious," Rachel said.

"Paul always looks serious except when he's around you," Maggie said as she hurried to open the door. "Paul, it's freezing out there. Where's your topcoat?"

"I don't own one," he replied with a sheepish grin.

"I'll get you a cup of coffee." Maggie headed for the kitchen.

"You're not dressed," Paul observed as he came into the living room and sat down.

"You certainly are," Rachel replied as she wrapped her housecoat more tightly around her legs.

Maggie returned with the coffee. "I'll just be upstairs," she said, and escaped the charged atmosphere of the room.

"You should hurry. We don't want to be late," Paul observed as he sipped the coffee.

"For what?" Rachel eyed him with suspicion. His nonchalance did not fool her. In fact, it made her more certain that he—and possibly her sisters—were up to something.

"Church."

"Church?" It was a laughable idea. "You?"

"And you," he replied. "And Maggie and Sara and probably Doc and a host of others who make this a regular part of their Sunday routine."

"It's been a very long time since church was a part of your Sunday routine."

He shrugged. "I thought I'd give it another shot."

She turned away from him and stared out the window.

"Maybe you should give it a shot, as well," he suggested as if it didn't matter to him one way or another.

"You don't find God in church, Paul. You find Him in here." She touched the place where her heart beat. She heard him get up from the rocker and move closer.

"You know you don't want to miss this," he said softly, standing just behind her chair. "Think of it, Rachel—the surprised faces, the muffled whispers."

"Why are you doing this?"

He knelt next to her where she could see his face. "Because I think you aren't going because you know the first time will be hard. You know everyone will be looking at you, wondering about you, making up their own predictions about how you're *really* doing."

He had hit the nail on the head. Not returning to church had little to do with her sudden absence of faith. She had discovered that it was easy enough to fake piousness and pretend reverence. No, Rachel had avoided church as she had any public forum because she didn't think she could handle the looks of pity, the whispered comments about how she was so young and her future had been so bright.

"If I go with you," Paul continued, "then people won't know where to look first. They'll be so shocked to see me there that your presence will seem normal by comparison."

It was a gift. A wonderful gift from one friend to another. She understood that, and her heart filled with love for this gentle, kind man.

"Besides," he added with a grin, "it'll be fun. I mean, imagine Mrs. Spencer's face—and that's just for starters."

She couldn't stop the giggle that bubbled from somewhere deep inside. Maxine Spencer had made it clear that in her opinion Paul had besmirched—her exact word—his dear mother's memory by refusing to come back into the fold. Every time she saw Paul on the street or at some function, she gave him a look that left no doubt of her low opinion of him.

"She'll be beside herself," Rachel gasped through her giggles.

"And then, of course, there's the good reverend himself. He's been working so hard at this—"

"Now, that's just mean," she reprimanded him. "Pastor Griffith's heart is in the right place, and you know it."

"But even so, it's going to make his day, seeing me there."

She couldn't deny that.

"Come on, Rachel. Get dressed and come with me," he urged.

All of a sudden it was as if she could feel a weight

lifting. "Okay," she said, and smiled. "Okay," she repeated with more conviction.

"Great." He stood up and fetched her walker for her. "Maggie," he shouted. "She's coming up."

He walked with her to the stairs and helped her settle herself on the elevator chair. "Going up," he announced as he pressed the controls to send her on her way.

"See you in a few minutes," she assured him, and she felt excited for the first time since the accident. She glanced down and saw Paul watching her ascend the stairs. She couldn't read his expression. There was something pensive about it and more. It was the more that she didn't understand.

Maggie helped her dress for church. As Rachel brushed her hair, she caught a glimpse of the sweatshirt she'd been wearing a few days earlier. Was the miracle that Paul was actually going to go to church? Rachel smiled at her reflection and felt more lighthearted than she had in weeks. She'd give God one thing—getting Paul McCoy to darken the door of a church was certainly miracle material.

By the time they arrived at the church almost everyone was already inside. They could hear the strains of the organ as they entered the vestibule. Rachel had persuaded Maggie and the others to go on ahead and save seats for Paul and her.

"Ready?" Paul asked after he'd hung up her coat. She had insisted on using her walker rather than the chair.

She nodded and swallowed hard. It felt strange to be here in the church again, not because the church had changed, but because everything about her was different.

"That's my girl," he whispered as he pulled open the door to the sanctuary. He let her go ahead of him. "I'm right behind you," he told her as she took one tentative step.

She saw their faces first—the eyes widening as she made her way up the center aisle. Maggie and Sara had gone to the family's usual pew near the front. It seemed a very long distance to walk pushing the hated walker. She began to regret that she hadn't insisted on her chair, but Paul had reminded her that the chair would elicit even more pity than the walker. She pasted a bright smile on her face and moved forward.

Then, as Paul had predicted, she saw all eyes shift to him. She even heard a few gasps of surprise, and Maxine Spencer looked as if she might actually pass out. The fake smile blossomed into a real one as she realized that together they had pulled it off. Hardly anyone seemed to notice as she slid into the pew, but even Pastor Griffith's bushy eyebrows fluttered when Paul slid in next to her, folded his hands piously and gave his full attention to the minister's opening words.

"The psalmist records in Psalm Twenty-five, verse four, the following message." The preacher's voice boomed over the suddenly hushed congregation. "'Direct me in Your ways, Yahweh, and teach me Your paths.'"

Rachel leaned forward, her attention focused on the words. It was as if she had a great thirst and was looking for something to quench it.

"In Psalm Forty-three, verse five, the psalmist raises an important question. 'Why so downcast, why all these sighs?' he asks. 'Hope in God! I will praise Him still, my savior, my God.' Let us all rise and join in the singing of hymn number eighty-four."

It seemed to Rachel that Pastor Griffith looked directly at her as he quoted this last passage and then announced the first hymn. It was an old favorite that Rachel knew by heart. It was hard not to sing along.

As the organist played the introduction and the congregation stood, she felt Paul put his arm around her, helping her stand, giving her his strength to lean against as they shared the hymnal she held.

Paul sang, too, his voice tentative as he searched for the melody. Rachel sang by rote, her mind focused on the verse the preacher had just quoted. *Why so downcast, why all these sighs?*

Why, indeed. She looked around her and saw a church filled with people who would count her as their friend or at the very least as their neighbor. She glanced to her left and saw Maggie, singing lustily, and Sara, more sedate, but nonetheless involved in the moment. She thought of her brothers off at college, sending her funny cards in Dallas and calling her now that she was home. She thought of the Wilsons and all they had done. She thought of Doc.

Most of all, she felt Paul's arm encircling her waist, felt his strength pouring into her, helping her stand without need of the walker for the duration of the hymn. *Why all these sighs?* She was truly blessed, surrounded by people she could count on to help her in times of need and to rejoice with her in times of celebration.

She felt a tear form at the corner of her eye, but it was not a tear of pain or despair. It was a tear of relief. If she was to recover her faith, she needed to listen, to pay attention to the world around her, to look beyond her own pain and see what was needed by others. As far as she could see there was no better place to start that process than here, in the third pew on the left on a wintry Sunday morning with her family and Paul at her side.

Paul felt her straighten, felt beneath his supporting hand the lengthening of her spine. He glanced at her and saw that she had entered wholeheartedly into the singing, where only seconds before her effort had been far less enthusiastic.

Maybe it was the way the light of the winter morning was spilling through the transom of the stained-glass window and spotlighting her glorious hair. Maybe it was the smile, the rapture in her gaze as she looked straight at the minister, but something had changed. She glowed, and the radiance came from within. He thought he had never seen her look more beautiful and he thought his heart would burst from loving her so deeply.

*Thank You,* he thought subconsciously as the last chords of the hymn died away. There was a general rustling of clothing and hymnbooks reshelved in racks on the backs of the pews as people settled into their seats. Paul was the last to sit, mostly because he was thunderstruck to realize that he had uttered a prayer. On top of that, it wasn't the first prayer he had spoken since Rachel's accident. In giving thanks he was acknowledging that his earlier prayers had been heard—and answered.

He barely heard the words of the sermon, was barely aware that twice more he stood with Rachel to sing God's praises. He was only aware of her, of the fact that something had changed for both of them by bringing her here. He felt for the first time since receiving that phone call in the airport that she was going to be all right.

The strains of the last hymn faded, and once more

the minister stepped to the podium, holding out his hand in a gesture of blessing as he quoted one more verse.

"And the psalmist entreats us in Psalm Thirty-three, verse three, to 'Sing to him a new song, make sweet music for your cry of victory.' And let us say together, amen."

Paul glanced at Rachel and knew that the words were illustrative of what would happen in her life. Rachel would find that new song and she would triumph. For a moment he was afraid he might cry as he realized that. He bowed his head and said amen, with the others, and perhaps for the first time in a decade, he meant it.

After church they were besieged by friends and neighbors who had not had a chance to see Rachel since her return from Dallas. All of them marveled over how well she looked, what progress she had made and how the doctors must be amazed at her recovery. Rachel received each compliment with a smile. She listened patiently as several people related tales of their own or a family member's illness or tragedy, and knew that in listening she was giving them something. One of the things that had upset her most about her accident was the constant need to receive the gifts of time and effort and caring from others and her seeming inability to give anything in return other than her gratitude. It didn't seem to be enough, and that had frustrated her.

"I understand now that it was an underlying cause of my anger," she told Paul later that afternoon as they sat together in the living room.

"I'm afraid I don't," Paul confessed.

"Don't you see? I kept trying to give back tit for tat—if you did something for me then I *had* to do something for you in return."

"Sounds rational."

"Life isn't all that rational, though. The fact is I achieve the same thing—in fact, I achieve more—by turning around and giving something of myself to someone who is more needy than I am. I take the kindness or the healing or the talent that you or Jan or Maggie share with me and I find my own version of that to give to someone else. Like when Sami gets here—I'll be helping him."

"But you give back to others all the time. You do that through just being you, through your teaching and your music."

She dismissed that idea with an impatient wave of her hand. "Making music is a lovely thing. It brings a moment of contentment or peace perhaps to some people at some particular moment. What I'm talking about is focus—a new song, as the psalm says. Maybe my calling is using my music to help others—not a big-time ministry, as I had once imagined, but in smaller doses."

Paul still looked puzzled.

Rachel grinned. "The truth is that I don't really entirely get it myself yet, but for the first time in weeks, I'm sure that I'm on the right track, Paul. I can feel His presence. What I need to do is think about my life in a new way. This accident happened for a reason, and what I need to do is figure out what it is that God intends for me to learn as a result."

"Just remember that sometimes God is a cruel teacher," Paul said, and held up his hands to forestall her protest. "I know what you think, but the fact is that an eighth of an inch in the way you fell and you could have ended up paralyzed for life."

"Oh, Paul, don't you see? That's just it—He made sure there was that eighth of an inch difference."

# *Chapter Thirteen*

The boy was rail thin and missing one leg from the knee down, yet he walked along on his prosthesis with something close to a swagger. He had a mop of brown hair and enormous dark-chocolate-fudge-colored eyes that constantly scanned the room even as they seemed focused only on the person he was with. His smile came easily, and he had a distinctive deep throaty laugh that was not in keeping with a boy of his size. Rachel knew immediately that this had to be Sami.

"Rachel," Jan called to her from across the room. "Come and meet the newest member of our little community here."

As Rachel made her way slowly across the room using her walker for support, she saw Sami studying her, sizing her up. His gaze lingered on her legs and the walker.

"Sami, this is Rachel Duke. I believe the two of you have exchanged some letters," Jan said.

Rachel held out her hand. "It's great to meet you at last, Sami. Welcome to Smokey Forge."

"Why is it that you use the metal thing?" he asked.

"It's something I need until I can get a little stronger," Rachel explained.

"Can you play your guitar or do you need to sit down for that?"

"I..."

"Sami," Jan warned.

Sami's attention remained on Rachel. There was no malice in him. His attitude was simply one of open curiosity.

"I haven't really thought about it," Rachel admitted. "It's been a while since I played."

The dark eyes grew even larger. "But your accident was weeks ago. Dr. Paul told me himself. Does it hurt to play?" His English was perfect.

She knew he was asking about physical pain. "I've had other things on my mind," she answered lamely.

"Well, I cannot wait to resume my soccer career," he announced. "I will work every day as much as I can until I am once again able to score the goal."

Both Jan and Rachel worked hard to hide their smiles at his assumption that playing soccer was for him a career rather than a schoolyard activity. "Really?" Rachel said.

"Oh, yes. I met a doctor at the hospital where they did my surgery, and he said that it was most important for me to get an early start and practice. This is even though other doctors have said I will not play again. You had surgery, didn't you?"

"Yes, I did, Sami."

"And now you must work very hard to get back to your career, as well. We can do this together, don't you think?"

Rachel stared at him. He had been told—as she had—

that his recovery would not be total. He had heard that and refused to accept it, at least until it could be proven. It occurred to her that the difference between her and Sami was that she had heard her doctors say she would never walk independently again and accepted it.

"Out of the mouths of babes," she said softly to herself, and saw that Sami was still waiting expectantly for her response to his challenge.

"We will work together, yes?"

Paul arrived before Rachel could form an answer. "I told you he was direct," he reminded her. "Well, Samir, my friend, have you managed to get everything reorganized around here?"

The boy laughed. "You are a kidder, Dr. Paul." He wagged one finger at Paul, but continued to smile. "Ms. Rachel Duke and I are becoming acquainted."

"And how is that going?" Paul looked at Rachel, then back to Sami.

"Quite well, would you not say so?"

"Very well," Rachel hastened to add.

"And now, if it will not displease you, Ms. Jan Stokes will begin my session. We have much work to do, yes?"

"Yes," Jan agreed with a laugh.

She walked to the opposite end of the room, and Sami followed her, swinging along jauntily on his crutches.

"He's incredible," Rachel said softly.

"He's determined, too. I wouldn't take that business about becoming a soccer star lightly. He's dead serious. He believes that that would be his ticket for staying in the States."

"I wouldn't think of belittling his dream," Rachel assured Paul.

"What about your dreams?" he asked as they watched Sami begin his workout with Jan.

"I told you—I'm rethinking them."

She saw the dismay in Paul's expression and laughed. "It's not a bad thing, Paul," she assured him. "I just need to figure things out now that I find myself in this new place in my life. Perhaps I'll talk to Sami. Clearly, he's very good at figuring things out."

"Well, all I know is that he made you smile, and that's good enough for me."

Rachel stayed much longer than usual at the center that day. At first she got caught up in observing Sami working through his session. After an hour of what Rachel knew had to be painful work, he took a break while Jan worked with another patient.

"How's it going?" Rachel asked. She knew that Sami had not seen her approach. He had been lost in his own thoughts and for the first time all morning his expression was pensive, even a little apprehensive.

"Fine. All right. Good."

The smile was firmly locked into place, but Rachel knew better than to believe the smile. She searched his eyes. "I was watching you. It's hard work."

He nodded and fought to keep up the cheerful facade.

"Does it hurt? Your leg, I mean."

"It's going to be okay," he assured her, but his voice trembled slightly.

"Sometimes my back hurts so much that I don't think I can stand it one more minute, much less for a whole hour."

His eyes widened.

"Sometimes," she confided, lowering her voice to a confidential whisper, "I wish I could just stay in bed and never have to lift a weight or do another exercise."

She saw that he wanted to trust her, confide in her. She certainly wouldn't blame him if he decided against it. After all he'd been through, it was a miracle that he would let anybody come near him. He was used to being strong for his family. She understood that it would be hard to let down his guard.

"Sometimes I feel that way," he admitted, and his voice was barely audible, "but then…" He didn't seem to know how to finish the thought.

"It's okay, you know. It's really hard being strong all the time, being the one everybody depends on. Even grown-up people have to lay down their burden and rest every once in a while."

"Like Dr. Paul?"

"Sure."

"I always knew he'd send for me."

"He's thought about you every day since he left," Rachel assured him.

Sami nodded. "I just wish…"

"Say it, Sami. Tell me what you wish, and maybe we can find a way to make it happen."

"I worry about my sisters," he whispered. "My aunt is a good person, but she is not their mother and she is young herself and…"

"Let me talk to Dr. Paul and see what we can do."

Instantly his face was alive with excitement. "Really? You can do this?"

"I can talk to Paul. There are no promises beyond that. I know that you understand that, Sami."

He nodded. "I know," he replied in a tone resigned to the frustrating ways of the world. Then he smiled. "But Dr. Paul can do wonderful things."

Rachel smiled. "Yes, he can. Dr. Paul can indeed do

wonderful things." She held out her arms to Sami, and he came to her.

Paul found them that way, holding on to each other, their whispered conversation making him wonder what these two might be plotting. Their laughter told him that it was probably something major.

"Well, you two have clearly hit it off," he said after Sami had left the room with Jan for a session of aquatic therapy.

"He is more wonderful than I imagined, Paul. We have to help him."

"We are helping him. He's here. He's had the surgery he needed and now he's getting the rehabilitation that will make him capable of things he couldn't even have dreamed of back there."

"He wants to bring his sisters here, and we have to see if we can make that happen."

Paul looked away.

"What is it?" Rachel's voice shook with anxiety. "Tell me they are all right. Please, don't say that something has happened to his sisters."

"They're fine. At least as far as I know. It has nothing to do with his sisters. You have to understand that we can't bring every kid over here just because they need to get out of there." He sounded frustrated and edgy, and she realized that since she'd come home, they hadn't really talked as they had before the accident. She accepted her role in that. He'd been trying to keep her spirits up, and so, of course, would not tell her any bad news.

"Then what is it? Don't protect me, Paul. Tell me what's bothering you."

It was the last thing he had wanted to do, but he knew

that he had to tell somebody. No, not just somebody. He wanted to tell Rachel.

"It's the funding for the center."

"What about it?"

"We used the donation from the Wilsons to outfit the van and update the heating and plumbing on the old hospital building. For this, we had to borrow." His hand swept the room, indicating the renovation and the expensive equipment. "And there's more to do if we're really going to build this into a workable program."

"You can't give up, Paul. This is your dream coming true."

"Expensive dream," he said wryly.

"What about grant money?"

"It'll come, but it takes time. Meanwhile, we have loans to pay with interest plus the day-to-day running of the program. It's possible that we may need to cut back on the services we planned to offer—at least until we can get the grant funding."

Rachel knew how hard it was to get grant funding. She'd watched Sara agonize over it often enough in trying to fund programs for the school. "Are you saying you might have to shut down?"

"No, we can do it, but we have to proceed within our means. We simply can't add bringing more kids out of Kosovo and other such places on top of everything else. As crass as it sounds, we may need to seek out some paying customers—some families who have insurance so we can get this place on its feet first."

"What about the kids like Henry and Sami and all the others? They're the reason you started this in the first place."

"That's pretty much the catch-22. We were in line for this one government grant, but then the program got cut. It was a five-year grant, and we were counting on it.''

"Oh, Paul, I'm so sorry. What can I do?"

He handed her the walker that was always close at hand. "First, get well. I need you around to help me."

"And?"

He sobered. "And don't get Sami's hopes up about his sisters. There's no medical reason to bring them here that we know of, and right now I need to spend all my time just keeping this place running so Sami can stay here and get the help he needs."

"There must be something I can do," she insisted as he walked with her to the strength-building weight machines.

"You're doing it," he assured her when she had settled into place for the first exercise. "Just get well." He touched the tip of her nose and then waved to Sami and Jan as he left the room.

That night, Sami came to supper with Paul and Doc. He didn't even have to work at charming Maggie, and Sara had him enrolled in the school almost as soon as he came through the door.

"I can be in your music lessons," he announced happily to Rachel at dinner. "I know your songs. Dr. Paul has played them for me in a…how do you say it? CD?"

Everyone else glanced nervously at Rachel. No one had dared raise the question of her music since the night of the Christmas party in Dallas. Doc cleared his throat.

"Well, now, son…"

"I think it would be a wonderful thing if you came into the school choir," Rachel said, focusing her attention on Sami but aware of the reactions of the others. "You don't have to know my songs to qualify. You just have to come to rehearsal on time."

"I can do that. I am very good at time." He held up his thin arm to show off a giant wristwatch.

Everyone laughed and relaxed a little.

"Are you saying you plan to return to teaching?" Paul asked her when the laughter had died.

It was Rachel's turn to laugh and put them all at ease once again. "Well, I would say it's about time I earned my keep around here, wouldn't you?"

Maggie started to cry, Sara became overly involved in clearing the table, and Paul just stared at her as if she had suddenly announced she was planning to try out for the Olympics.

Doc reacted as he had always reacted when life dealt him a pleasant surprise. "I think that's a real good idea, Rachel, honey. A *real* good idea." He reached over and covered her hand with both of his and squeezed to let her know how much she had touched them all.

"The children are going to be so happy," Maggie blubbered through her tears.

"This is a sad thing?" Sami whispered to Paul as he observed the gamut of emotions.

"No, a glad thing. Sometimes people—especially women—like to cry even when they're happy."

"Confusing," Sami muttered and frowned. "I can still be in the choir?"

"Definitely," Rachel assured him and put her arm around him. She noticed that he immediately curled into her embrace, becoming the little boy that he was for the first time since she'd met him. She felt him tremble and understood that the effort he made to convince everyone that he was in charge was even more exhausting for him than her emotional journey had been for her.

Watching them, Paul found himself thinking about what it might be like if he and Rachel were to marry and settle here in Smokey Forge. After all, even if she were to return to performing some day, it would be some time. Her rehabilitation was going well, but it would have to be accomplished in stages. Once she could give up the wheelchair and even the walker, there was still a great deal of work to be done.

He found himself playing the game he'd picked up from her—the what-if game. What if she could learn to love him instead of looking upon him as just a friend who used to have a thing for her sister? What if they could make a life together? Have children together? What if the way to help Sami and his sisters was to bring them all to live with him and Rachel?

*Whoa,* he thought. *You of all people have never been the settling down type and now you're thinking not only about a wife, but a ready-made family?*

"Isn't that right, Paul?"

He looked blankly at Maggie, realizing that conversation had gone on while he'd been lost in thought.

"I'm sorry. I was..."

"Not listening," Maggie chided him in her best schoolmarm voice. "I was saying that I thought it would be a great welcome back for Rachel if the children performed a concert on the day she returns to teach."

Paul glanced at Rachel and saw that she was okay with this. "I think it's a very good idea," he told Maggie. "Can I come?"

"Of course," Sara told him. "And Doc, as well."

It was on that first day back at school that a plan for helping save the center first took form in Rachel's mind. Not that she had anticipated any such idea in this particular setting. Mostly, she was concentrating on not being overwhelmed by the excitement of the children at her return. They were all at the windows of their classroom when she arrived at the school, their faces pressed against the cold glass as they watched her wheel herself up the ramp that had always been there to accommodate any students or staff with disabilities. Rachel had never imagined that the ramp might be for her.

As she wheeled herself slowly toward the front entrance, she thought about all the times she'd used the ramp as a shortcut to her car in the parking lot or when she was late for a lesson. Those times she had run up or down the ramp never giving a thought to how it might be to navigate the ramp in a wheelchair or on crutches. She had never thought about the steepness of the slope of it until now.

Even later, as she sat in the front row of the school's small auditorium, it did not occur to her that later in the morning she would have an epiphany that would change her life forever. Her attention was on the children, the eighteen members of the school's choir. Maggie and Sara had impressed upon her how hard the children had worked on this and how important it was to them.

The children were dressed in their Sunday best and stood in three semi-straight lines on the low platform that served as a stage. One by one, they sang the songs she had taught them—spirituals, favorite hymns, songs she had learned in her own days in Bible school. Sara accompanied them at the piano, and Maggie directed.

As she listened, Rachel felt something happening inside her. There was a loosening of the tight knot that had occupied the center of her being ever since the accident. In truth, the knot had been there even before the accident. Throughout the tour she had felt it binding her, tightening its hold on her, changing her shape, her outlook. Even Paul had been unable to loosen it—although he had tried, and she loved him for his willingness to risk her anger to help her.

She turned her attention to the children. A choir of angels could not have made more beautiful music than those marvelous children did as they turned old standards into heavenly anthems. She recognized her own part in this concert. She had arranged the music in keys all the children could sing. She had taught them the simple harmonies. She had choreographed the hand motions they used. It was a wonderful performance and a fantastic welcome back to the school for Rachel. Listening to them, she understood that she had made some small difference in the lives of these children. Perhaps she could make a difference for others, as well. Somehow there had to be a way for her to help Paul get the money he needed to keep the program going and help those children who most needed its services.

At the end of the last number, Rachel clapped and cheered as the children took their bows. She saw Maggie and Sara exchange nervous looks, then Sara's mouth tightened. With a look of resolution, she turned to the piano and launched into the introduction to Rachel's song "This Little Child."

Before Maggie could react, the children in the choir had straightened and started to sway from side to side in rhythm to the music. Rachel felt her chest tighten. The blood rushed to her cheeks. She didn't know where to look or what to do. She had the greatest urge to flee but knew that she couldn't. She would have to get through this moment. Her sisters intended no harm. They only wanted to help, but as far as she'd come, she wasn't ready for this—not yet.

"This one, I also know," Sami shouted excitedly. He

grabbed his crutches and rushed forward to join the other children, mounting with ease the two steps to the platform. Sara continued to play the introduction until he had found a place. In seconds he was leaning on his crutches and swaying with the others. The other children were startled at first, but then they closed ranks around him, including him in their circle as they turned their attention to Maggie.

Sara and Maggie exchanged looks and smiled broadly as Maggie gave the children the downbeat to begin the song. On the chorus Maggie turned and invited all those in attendance to join in, and the hall was filled with the joyous strains of Rachel's music. Rachel looked around and saw everyone singing—the children, their teachers and Paul standing by the door.

When the number was finished, there was a moment in which it seemed that every eye was on Rachel. Paul had not wanted to disturb the concert already in progress when he was finally able to get away from the center. He had watched her enjoy the children, her face luminous with delight. When he realized that Maggie and Sara intended to conclude with Rachel's song, he had resisted the urge to rush forward and protect Rachel from the pain of hearing her own music performed by others.

Then Sami had suddenly leaped up and joined the others, and Paul had thought that it would be enough to diffuse the moment. As Maggie turned and indicated that everyone should sing along, Paul saw Rachel turning in her chair, taking in the happy faces of the other students and teachers singing along. The expression on her face had been unreadable—a mixture of bewilderment and amazement. She turned slowly to face the stage as the song ended. Paul rushed forward and saw that she was crying.

The whispers spread through the audience as the children realized that she was sobbing. Sara and Maggie started toward Rachel, but Paul waved them off. He took the seat vacated by Sami and resisted the urge to pull her into his arms.

"Rachel?"

She motioned him away and buried her chin deeper into her chest as her shoulders shook with her crying.

Paul glanced helplessly toward the stage, looking to Maggie but finding instead that Sami was moving forward to take charge.

"It is not a sad thing," Sami announced, standing tall to talk into the microphone that Maggie had used to introduce each song. "People—especially the women—like to cry for happiness," he assured everyone. "This is happy even though it may seem sad. It is really quite confusing," he finished lamely and stepped back from the microphone.

Rachel was the first to start laughing. Her sobs gradually changed to giggles and then peals of laughter. When Paul saw that, he started to smile and then to laugh, as well. Then everyone was laughing, except for Sami, who looked a little bewildered but decided these crazy Americans must do things this way. Soon his deep foghorn laugh could be heard above the laughter of the others.

Sara struck up the chorus of Rachel's song, and everyone sang along. With Paul's help, Rachel stood and joined in on the chorus.

And God was there
And God could see

This little child
Was really me.

Paul didn't even care if he was off-key. He had never in his life felt more like singing. Rachel was filled with the pure pleasure of singing her own song again. Added to the commitment she had already made to return to teaching, Paul understood that he no longer needed to worry about Rachel Duke.

Not that he had ever doubted that she would find her way back. But he couldn't deny moments of skepticism. If Rachel, of all people, were to lose her way, then what possible hope could there be for the rest of them? It was Rachel he had come to count on to find the good in any adversity. In the absence of his own faith, he had come to depend upon the presence of hers to help him make it through the chaos of his own life. The fall and all its aftermath had left her reeling, and in her confusion, she had seemed ready to cast aside any facet of her life that seemed to have anything to do with the accident—including her beloved music. If she could regain her love of music and teaching, then he was sure that she would fully reclaim her faith.

He looked at her as they sang one last chorus. She moved in time to the music, joining the children in the hand choreography she had taught them. Her music not only touched others—after all these weeks it had finally touched her, as well.

"Welcome home," he whispered when the song ended and she hugged him.

She looked startled at first, and then he saw understanding dawn. "I don't know why I thought I needed to leave—there's far too much to be done here for me to even think of going anywhere else,'' she replied and hugged him again.

''I couldn't agree more,'' he whispered as he pulled her tightly into his embrace.

# Chapter Fourteen

Rachel could hardly wait for her session with Jan to end so that she could talk to Paul. She had come up with an idea that just might work for raising the funds to bring more children to the center.

"You're really making progress," Jan told her, and she sounded impressed. This was no pep talk. This was genuine respect.

Rachel wiped her face and arms with a towel. These days she approached her therapy as if it were a good workout. She could see the results. She was able to do things that even a week earlier she could not have done. She was determined to make it all the way back. "I'm feeling a little stronger every day, and I owe so much to you."

"No. You owe it to yourself and your willingness to do the work in spite of the pain," Jan replied. "I have to tell you that when we first met, I was very worried about you. Some of my clients lose the will to do the work, especially those who—like you—know there's only so far you can go. Frankly, I would have pegged you as one of them.''

Rachel laughed. "And you would have been right."

"What happened?"

"I realized that I had things to do and the best way to get them done was to get this business taken care of as quickly as possible so I could get on with my life. Putting it bluntly, I realized that I didn't want to give one more day to this than was necessary to achieve recovery.'' She pulled herself out of her wheelchair and made another trip up and down the stairs she had been unable to tackle two weeks earlier. "How much longer?" she asked Jan.

"Before your therapy is finished?"

"No, before I can graduate from the walker to a cane," Rachel replied, and saw Jan wrestle with an answer that was both honest and kind.

"I... Look, Rachel, there are circumstances—"

"Because I am going to make it all the way back, Jan, and I want it to be a surprise for my family and especially for Paul, okay?"

"We'll do the best we can," Jan assured her, but Rachel could see that she was skeptical.

"That's all I'm asking." She threw the towel over one shoulder and headed for the shower, ignoring the wheelchair as she half-carried her walker. "I'll see you tomorrow. I've got to make some calls and then get to class."

Paul was confused. He'd just had a call from Ezra Wilson, checking to see how things were going with the traveling van. They had talked for several minutes about the van, about Rachel and about the Wilsons, then Ezra had ended the call, saying, "We'll be looking forward to seeing you all next week, okay?'' He'd hung up before Paul could ask what he was talking about. Clearly, Ezra thought that Paul knew.

"Dad? Are we planning to see Ezra and Jonah Wilson next week?''

"I'm not sure,'' Doc answered, "but it would sure be nice to have a chance to thank them in person for their generosity.''

"Ezra seems to think we're getting together next week.''

Doc shrugged. "Check with Rachel. Most likely, they've been in touch with her and she forgot to tell you.''

More likely she had been in touch with the Wilsons and not mentioned it because she was up to something, Paul thought.

"I'm going by the center to pick up Rachel and take her home.''

"Why don't you two go someplace nice for supper for a change? Someplace where you can talk without all of us around to interrupt?'' Doc suggested.

Paul had gotten to know his father pretty well since returning to Smokey Forge. He certainly knew when the man was up to something. "What's going on?'' he asked.

Doc handed him his jacket and pushed him toward the door. "Go ask Rachel.''

At the center he found Rachel and Jan laughing together over some silly quiz in a magazine. Rachel had just finished showering, judging by the damp tendrils of hair that framed her face.

"Good session?'' he asked.

"Great,'' Jan reported. "She's my star client.'' She helped Rachel put on her coat, and Paul noticed that

Jan winked at Rachel in the process. Was everybody in on whatever it was that Rachel was planning?

"Ready to go?" he asked.

"Ready." She smiled at him.

Two could play this game, he thought as he helped her into the car and then started to drive away from town instead of toward the house.

"Where are we headed?" she asked.

"Dinner. I'm finally collecting on that date even if I have to kidnap you to do it."

"Paul, I'm really not dressed for a restaurant," she protested, indicating her sweatpants and running shoes. "Stop by the house and let me change."

"You're dressed perfectly for where we're going," he assured her. "How was school today?"

He kept her engaged in small talk until they reached the roadside diner on the outskirts of town that was known for its hamburgers and onion and chive fries.

"I'll be right back," he said, leaving the engine running as he hurried inside.

Rachel noticed that it had started to snow. Large flakes stuck to the windshield and flashed white in the headlights of the car.

"Here," Paul said, handing her a large paper bag that steamed with the delicious odor of hot food. He opened his door and got in, balancing two large milk shakes in the process. "I thought we'd have a picnic," he said, looking very proud of himself.

"In spite of the fact that it's February—not to mention that it's snowing?"

"Details." He placed the milk shakes in the cup holders and shifted the car into gear. "Ready?"

"Now where are we going?" she asked.

"Not far." He turned the car toward town, drove

down the main street past the clinic and the rehab center, up the hill and past the school and on into the night. Along the way, he made small talk about his day at the clinic.

"Paul? The food is going to get cold."

"We're almost there," he assured her as he turned off the paved road onto the snow-covered gravel road that led to the mill.

Rachel smiled. "Oh," was all she said as she relaxed in the seat and enjoyed the rest of the ride. The mill was the perfect place to tell him about her idea.

Paul pulled the car close to the place where the water fell over a small dam. "Looks a lot different than it did when we first used to come here," he said as she took charge of unwrapping the food and putting straws in the milk-shake cups.

Rachel looked at the scene made light by the snow. "It's always been one of my favorite places. I wrote some of my best music here."

"Past tense?"

She smiled. "Okay, I wrote some of my best music *to date* here."

"Better." He took a bite of his burger. "I had a call from Ezra today."

"Really? What did he have to say?"

Paul took a long swallow of his milk shake. "Why don't you tell me? Why is Ezra planning a trip here next week and why would he think I knew all about it?"

"Oh, that," Rachel said as she wrestled with opening one of the small packets of ketchup she found in the bottom of the bag.

"Let me do that," Paul said, taking it from her. "Talk to me, lady. What's going on?"

"Well, what if I were to tell you that Ezra and Jonah recorded my holiday song?"

"Without your permission?"

"No. They asked while I was in Dallas. I figured why not. I certainly was in no mood to record anything, much less a holiday song."

"Okay, so they recorded your song. What's that got to do with coming here?"

"Well, suppose they put out the CD with the understanding that all royalties come to the center?"

Paul forgot to swallow. "You're kidding."

"Nope. What if I told you that to date—after just six weeks—it's still climbing the charts?"

"That's good, right?"

"Well, so far it adds up to a year's worth of that grant you didn't get because the program was cut. Is that good?" She took a bite of her burger and gave him a wide-eyed look.

"It's incredible. Oh, Rachel, do you understand what this means?"

"There's more."

"There can't be—this is everything."

"Well, I talked to somebody else today." She paused a beat. "Todd Mayfield."

Paul's euphoric mood was instantly extinguished. "Todd? Why would you— I mean— Todd?"

"We had some business to discuss."

"Such as?"

"Well, I had been kind of mulling over this idea, and then after I talked to Ezra, I knew I was on the right track and..."

"What's the idea?" Paul settled back and waited.

Rachel moved to the edge of her seat, her eyes sparkling like the newly fallen snow. "What if we were to work together for the children?"

"Meaning?"

"What if I wrote songs and put together concerts with the kids and Todd got them recorded and got play time for them on all the major stations and the money went into some sort of foundation or fund and we could start to use that money to bring in the most serious cases from overseas, from wherever, and we could give the kids the rehabilitation they need and..."

"Slow down a minute. Are you saying you're going back onstage? Back on tour?" His emotions turned upside down. He should be happy. She had come back— all the way back, at least emotionally. Wasn't that what he had wanted for her? *No. I want her here. I want her to be my wife and sing in the church choir and teach little kids Bible school songs.*

"Well, yeah, in a way, I guess I am talking about performing again." She looked confused, as if that hadn't occurred to her until now.

"I think that's great, songbird."

"Really?"

"Really."

She leaned against the door and folded her arms across her chest. "Then why don't I believe you?"

"Really, I..."

"You don't think I can do this, do you? You don't think I can get back out there. Well, let me tell you something, Dr. McCoy, I—"

"Stop shouting at me. I'm not saying you *can't* do this or that you *shouldn't* do this—"

"Now, who's shouting?"

"I'm not shouting. I'm just saying that..." He paused, looking for a finish to that statement.

"What?" she shouted in complete frustration. "Spit it out."

He focused his attention straight ahead, looking at the falling snow instead of at her. Then he turned and said, "I love you. I don't want you to leave again."

The only sound for the next full minute was the water cascading over the boulders. They stared at each other. Her mouth was open, but no sound came out. He waited.

"Well?" he asked finally, his voice hoarse with fright at how she might react.

"Why?"

"Why?" He might have expected anything but that.

"Why do you love me?" She frowned.

"Are you serious? You are the most— You make me— Do you want all the classic movie lines or what?"

"I want a little honesty."

"A man tells you he's head over heels for you and—"

"You never said that."

"I'm saying it now."

"Oh." She looked as if all the air had suddenly gone out of her lungs.

"How do you feel about me?"

"I— That is, we—"

Paul grinned. "Not easy, is it?"

"We're off the subject."

"I don't think so. How we feel about each other seems to me to be very relevant to the subject of whether or not you go traipsing around the country making CDs and doing concert tours while I'm back here running the center, which is a lot more complex than helping Dad at the clinic, by the way." He gulped air and wondered how she was able to ramble on in those long, intense sentences of hers without pausing for a breath.

"I never said I was going back on tour, and I try very hard not to *traipse* anywhere."

"Now who's changing the subject? It's a simple question, Rachel," Paul said, cutting through the banter they were both using to get them past the shock of his declaration. "I love you. Do you have feelings for me?"

"Yes, but..."

He put his fingers against her lips. "All I heard was yes. I'm going to kiss you now, Rachel, okay?"

She nodded.

They leaned toward each other. Their lips met, clung for one long moment, then released on a mutual sigh. Their foreheads touched and their fingers entwined. They sat that way for a long moment.

"That was nice," she said finally.

He chuckled. "I thought so."

"What do we do now?"

"Well, why don't I calm down and let you tell me exactly what you have in mind?"

For the next couple of hours they talked through the details of her idea. The more she talked, the more excited he became. It might work, and the best part was, she could do it all from Smokey Forge.

Maggie was the first to take note of the shift in their relationship.

"Something's different," she announced to Rachel at breakfast a few days later. "Paul is here so often that he might as well move in."

"He's always been here," Rachel replied calmly.

Maggie studied her for a long moment. "*You're* different."

"Well, yeah. I can walk some without the walker and pretty soon I won't need that elevator chair to get upstairs."

"I'm not talking about physically." She strolled around Rachel.

"You're making me nervous, Mags."

"You're in love with him, aren't you?" Maggie started to grin. "And more to the point, he's finally owned up to being in love with you. Well, hallelujah. It's about time. Sara!"

Sara came rushing into the room. "What's happened? Has something happened to Rachel?" She glanced from Maggie to Rachel, who was calmly eating her cereal. "Well?" she asked, impatient at being interrupted.

"Rachel and Paul are in love."

"We knew that, Maggie. We've known it for weeks."

"Yes, but now *they* know it."

Sara started to smile. "Really?" She turned her attention to Rachel. "Really and truly?"

"She's not admitting anything," Maggie said. "She's probably afraid we're going to interfere."

"Ya think?" Rachel said, deliberately using the slang that the kids were so fond of tossing around at school.

"We do *not* interfere," Sara argued. "We simply want what's best for you."

Rachel got up from the table and put her dishes in the sink. "Well, I've found it in Paul," she told them. Then she grinned and held out her arms to them, inviting a group hug.

"When's the wedding?" Maggie asked.

"Whoa. We're not that far down this road yet. Let's don't try to rush this along."

"Does this mean that Paul intends to stay in Smokey Forge?" Sara asked.

"He has a practice here now—the center? The traveling health van?"

"You'll stay home, as well," Maggie said, and Rachel could see that it was something she had been hoping for but afraid to bring up.

"For now, we're both here," Rachel assured her.

Throughout the day she thought about the question Maggie had raised. *When was the wedding?* She couldn't deny that it had crossed her mind. Under most circumstances, it was a logical step for two people in love. But was it logical for Paul and her? Was it even possible given their disparate views of life and the work God had given them to do?

It was clear that even though Paul seemed to have mellowed toward her faith in God, he had not embraced it for himself. He had not returned to church after that first Sunday, and while he accepted that her beliefs were a key to her recovery, he believed that it was the science of medicine and therapy that had brought her as far as she could come.

She had always thought that loving someone meant acceptance of the whole person, flaws and all. Trying to change another person would just destroy the relationship. On the other hand, helping a man find his way back to God might be the most loving thing she could ever do in her life, and if the relationship got sacrificed in the process, wasn't it worth it?

"No, God, it's not. Not this relationship, anyway," she argued as she worked out in her room, practicing walking without the aid of a walker or cane. "If he wants to marry, then I'm going to say yes, okay? You'll help me figure out the rest as we go along. No disrespect meant, but frankly bringing Paul back into the fold is really Your job, isn't it?'' She glanced toward the ceiling and waited. ''Okay, so I can be an instrument in that, but don't expect me to make it an ultimatum.''

A few days later, Paul was driving past the school on his way home from yet another meeting when he noticed the kid on the field and the woman on the sidelines. The typical parent-child scene tugged at his heartstrings. As usual it made him think of Rachel. Everything made him think of her these days.

As he got closer to the field, he realized that there was something familiar about the boy and the woman, and yet what he was seeing was impossible. He pressed on the gas, urging the car into the nearest parking space so he could get a better look.

Sami was on the field, his crutches propped against a bench on the sideline next to where Rachel sat. The boy was working a soccer ball down the field toward the goal. Occasionally, he lost control of the ball but resolutely chased it down. Paul could hear Rachel's shouts of encouragement through the closed car window.

''You're almost there, Sami. Twenty yards,'' she shouted. ''Ten.''

Paul got out of his car and moved toward the field, his heart hammering as he watched the child he thought would never be able to play his favorite sport again move steadily toward the goal.

''That's it,'' Rachel yelled. ''Come on. You can make it. Come on.''

Paul glanced over and saw that she was standing, her

body poised as if she were the one about to kick the goal. It took a moment to understand that she was standing without aid—no walker. No cane.

"You're there," she shouted. "The clock is running down. You have to make the winning goal. Five... four...three..."

Paul's attention swung to Sami. In amazement he watched as the boy sidekicked the ball straight into the net with his artificial leg. As the ball cleared the boundaries and caught the net, there was silence on the field, and then Sami and Rachel both exploded into cheers.

Still oblivious to his presence, they ran toward each other in an awkward hobbling manner but without aid. They met and caught each other in a bear hug, their voices hoarse with shouts of victory.

Paul watched it all, knowing it was a moment he would replay for the rest of his life. Whenever he felt that life was unfair, that the world was narrow-minded and biased, that there was no God, he would remember this moment. There was no medical reason either of them should be capable of moving this freely. He blinked, wondering if he was just tired and hallucinating, but when he opened his eyes, there they were, standing unaided in the middle of the field reliving the moment. Impossible as it was for him to accept, there was no scientific explanation. Something greater than mere medicine had healed them both.

"Thank You," he whispered, and fell to his knees, unable to stay upright in the presence of such a miracle. "Thank You for this." He almost added that he would never again ask for anything more, but knew that would not be true. In the years to come there would be many times when he would need help beyond his abilities to manage the trials of life, and he would turn—as he had even when he was in deepest denial—to God for help.

"Paul?"

He looked up and saw Rachel and Sami standing next to him. They both looked frightened. "Are you okay?" Rachel asked, and when she saw his tear-streaked face, she knelt next to him.

"You can walk," he said.

"And I can play," Sami added proudly. "One day I will score the winning goal for real, right, Rach?"

"Right." She ruffled his hair.

"But how?" Paul asked.

Rachel grinned at Sami and together they unzipped their ski jackets to reveal matching sweatshirts that read, Expect a Miracle.

# *Chapter Fifteen*

Rachel had been attending church regularly ever since the Sunday that Paul had baited her into going. She found what she had always found there—peace, solace and on this particular Sunday, cause for rejoicing. Sami was at her side. He was going to be all right, going to be able to play his beloved soccer. He was safe and whole and that was reason enough to praise God on this early March Sunday when the first hint of spring had flavored the morning breeze.

As she stood with the rest of the congregation for the opening hymn, she looked up to see Paul standing in the aisle waiting for her to make room for him. He gave her a sheepish grin as he took his place next to her, held one side of the hymnal and started to sing in his off-key baritone.

During the service, Rachel noticed that unlike the other Sunday, Paul concentrated on the minister's words. He read the congregational portion of the response reading with inflection and meaning. During the sermon, he sat slightly forward, his eyes riveted on Pastor Griffith as he listened to the message of the day.

Following the sermon there was quiet music for meditation followed by the announcements of church activities and meetings.

"Are there any further announcements?" Reverend Griffith asked, clearly expecting none.

"Yes." Paul raised his hand like one of the children in school and then stood.

"Well, Doctor, I..." Griffith faltered for words. "The floor is yours," he said finally.

Paul moved quickly up the aisle and faced the congregation. "When I was a boy, growing up in this church, there was a part of the service that was called Joys and Concerns."

Rachel saw people nodding throughout the congregation.

"People would come up here and talk about things that were happening in their life or to people they knew. Somebody was sick, somebody else had a new grandchild, that sort of thing."

The attention of every person in the church was focused on Paul.

"Well, the other day, I experienced one of the most joyous days of my life and pushing my luck—as most of you know I'm famous for doing—I'm going to try for a second such day right now."

Soft chuckles rippled through the pews as people whispered the explanation to others that Paul had always been something of a rebel—someone who marched to his own drummer. Rachel saw that for the most part people were very glad he had decided to do that again. They leaned toward him, their faces curious as they waited for whatever he might tell them.

Rachel assumed he was about to announce some major news about the clinic project. She looked at Sami and then at Paul.

"I would like to ask Ms. Rachel Duke to join me up here," he said quietly, his eyes on Rachel.

She reached for her cane, but Paul moved quickly down the aisle and took it from her. "You don't need this, remember?" he said softly as he hooked the curved handle of the cane over the end of the pew and offered her his hand instead.

Rachel stood as she accepted his hand and together they started down the aisle toward the pulpit. It was only when she heard the gasps of surprise and Maggie's muffled shout of rejoicing that she realized that Paul had released her hand and she was walking unaided.

"As I mentioned," Paul said when they had reached the front of the church and turned to face everyone, "I have already had a reason to rejoice this week." He told the story of seeing Rachel and Sami on the soccer field. "My good friends and neighbors, I need for you to understand and appreciate that there is no medical reason in the world why this happened. Rachel and Sami have both received the very best that medicine has to offer. Even so, they were not expected to ever be able to achieve what I witnessed this week on that soccer field and what you have just seen this morning."

The members of the congregation burst into spontaneous applause. People stood and cheered and whistled through their teeth. Paul motioned for them to be seated. Rachel could not imagine what was coming next.

"I told you that I hoped to recreate the joy I felt on that soccer field a few days ago. So here goes." He fumbled in his jacket pocket for a minute and then knelt on one knee. "Rachel Duke, you have changed my life.

You have taught me courage and conviction and tenacity. Most of all, you have reminded me that we are not in this alone. You have brought me home. I love you with all my heart.'' He opened the stiff-hinged lid of the tiny blue jeweler's box. ''Will you marry me?''

No one heard Rachel's reply, but when she flung herself into Paul's arms, they knew the answer was yes, and for the second time that morning, they stood as one and cheered.

''And let us all say together—amen,'' Pastor Griffith announced in the voice he used every Sunday for the benediction.

''Amen,'' the congregation replied, and it was Sami's foghorn voice that could be heard above everyone else's.

From the minute church ended, Rachel found herself in a whirlwind.

''There's so much to do,'' Sara announced immediately following the service.

''Well, it would be nice to start with a date,'' Maggie said, turning her attention to Rachel and Paul.

''The sooner the better.'' Paul looked at Rachel as if having gotten her agreement to marry him, he was ready to begin their life together immediately.

''How about April? I've always loved spring here in the mountains.'' Rachel looked to Paul for agreement.

''It could rain,'' Sara warned.

''Or not,'' Rachel replied dreamily. ''An outdoor wedding up at the house with everyone gathered like a big old-fashioned reunion or picnic. I think Mom and Dad would like that,'' she added as if she fully expected her parents to be there.

''All right, April it is,'' Sara agreed with a sigh. ''At

least that gives us some time—a little more than a year should give us plenty of time to…''

Paul and Rachel stared at her openmouthed.

"Not *next* April, Sara," Rachel corrected her. "*This* April."

Both Maggie and Sara looked startled. "That's less than a month away, honey," Maggie reminded her gently.

"I know, but the time will go quickly," Rachel assured Paul.

"Oh, my stars," Sara moaned. "Well, I'm going to talk to Pastor Griffith right now and check his calendar." She hurried away.

"I'd better see if Mabel Woodward can get the bridesmaids' dresses done in time," Maggie said as she hurried off in the opposite direction.

Paul and Rachel were alone for the first time all morning. "You are incredible," she told him. "What if I had said no?"

He shrugged and grinned. "Then I would have been pretty embarrassed. Even if you had said no I would have spent as long as it took to convince you. After all, I know you love me."

"Pretty cocky, aren't you?"

"And why not? The most beautiful, incredible woman in Smokey Forge just agreed to marry me. Life is good, lady."

"Where should we go on our honeymoon?" Paul asked later that night. They had escaped to the front porch swing, unable to take another minute of Maggie's and Sara's making minutely detailed lists for the wedding and reception.

Rachel pulled the blanket they'd wrapped around their shoulders closer. "How about Kosovo?"

Paul laughed. "Oh, yeah, now that's really romantic."

"I'm serious. What if we went there and got Sami's sisters out?"

He was quiet for a long moment, but she knew him well enough by now to understand that he was actually considering the possibility.

"We'd have to have a very good reason."

"How about adoption?" she asked.

"You mean someone here adopting them?"

"I was thinking maybe we would adopt them—and Sami, too, of course." She turned her head and looked at him. "Could you handle a wife plus a ready-made family?"

"You don't have to do this, Rachel. We'll find a way to get them out."

"I want to do it—if you agree. I've been so blessed in my life, and think of the family we would be giving them. Maggie and Sara, not to mention Doc. Can you see him as a grandfather? He'd be absolutely wonderful."

"Maybe C.R. and Emma would agree to be godparents," Paul added, catching her excitement. "Do you really think I could be a good father?"

"I think you would be a wonderful father. You've already proven that with Sami. He adores you."

Paul grinned. "I'm kind of partial to the little guy myself."

"So we honeymoon in Kosovo?"

"Sounds like a plan. I'll start making the arrangements."

They were quiet for a moment, rocking gently in the

porch swing as they enjoyed the night with its promise
of spring.

"Maggie and Sara are going to have a bird when we
tell them this," Rachel said with a giggle.

"Let's go tell them now. I can't wait to see their
faces. I'll be very casual—'Oh, by the way, Rachel and
I just decided on the honeymoon location.' They're going to think we've gone completely mad."

"But when they think about it, they'll be thrilled at
the prospect of being aunties. They already spoil Sami
shamelessly."

To their amazement, both sisters took the news in
stride.

"Anything else?" Sara asked in her no-nonsense
manner.

"Not at the moment," Paul replied.

"Good." Maggie sighed with relief. "I don't think I
can handle any more surprises tonight."

The mountains were garbed in their spring finery on
the day that Rachel married Paul. A predawn shower
had left everything sparkling and fresh. The ceremony
took place as planned, outside the Duke house. The
wedding party walked down the front porch steps and
into the yard through a bower covered with flowers entwined in dried grapevines. Serving together as Rachel's
maids of honor, Maggie and Sara were dressed in ecru
lace with forest-green satin sashes tied in a bow with
streamers to the hem of their ankle-length gowns. They
carried bouquets of deep green and rose mountain laurel
spiked with twigs of pink and white dogwood. Rachel
wore her mother's wedding gown with the shawl from
Paul's mother tied around her shoulders. Her bouquet
was made up of three white lilies and cascades of bridal

wreath the sisters had picked from the yard fresh that morning.

The Wilson Brothers sang, and Doc sniffed back tears as he prepared to walk Rachel down the aisle to where Paul waited by the altar. C.R. served as the best man, and Sami and Henry proudly carried small white lace pillows with the rings tied in place by a satin ribbon.

As Paul watched Rachel appear at the top of the porch steps on the arm of his father, he looked heavenward and said softly, "Thanks, God, for sticking with me and bringing me to this place, this woman."

C.R. gave him a cockeyed smile.

Rachel saw Paul look at her and then at the blue sky above. She saw his mouth move and laughed happily. Throwing her head back so she could see the same blue sky, she said, "What he said, God, goes double for me."

Reverend Griffith delivered the traditional service, but everyone in attendance knew that he had never meant the words more sincerely than he did on this day. "And as Rachel and Paul share a kiss to seal their vows, let us all say together, amen."

\* \* \* \* \*

Dear Reader,

As I write this, it is snowing here in my Wisconsin home, one of those made-for-TV snows—light and fluffy and blessedly silent. 'Tis the season of miracles.

I had a miracle of my own this year. Last spring, just as I was beginning the final writing of *The Doctor's Miracle,* I was diagnosed with uterine cancer. In the most harrowing two weeks of my life, I went from being one of those people who has always been blessed with perfect health to having cancer, having surgery and starting down that long road to recovery. I thought there was no way I could focus on writing—especially a story about illness!

However, I found that writing this book was incredibly therapeutic. I looked at these characters with fresh eyes and a unique understanding. I thought about all of the miracles that had come to me in the form of this terrible diagnosis—friends and family, of course, but also doctors and nurses and co-workers and strangers who helped me face a moment of crisis and come away whole. I hope that you will also find a message of hope and healing in these pages.

Blessings,

Anna Schmidt

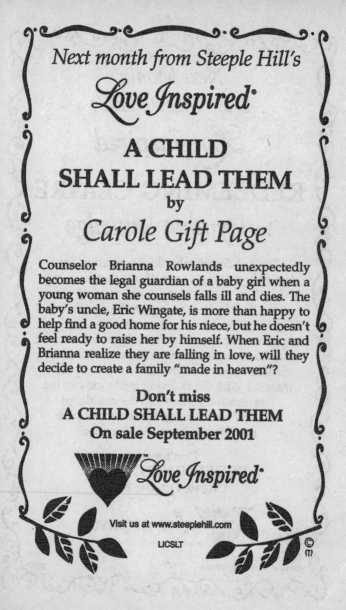

Next month from Steeple Hill's

*Love Inspired*

# TWIN BLESSINGS
### by

## Carolyne Aarsen

*Stable, responsible Logan Napier has his hands full trying to raise his twin ten-year-old nieces by himself. In desperate need of a tutor for them, Logan hires unconventional free spirit Sandra Bachman. Convinced their uncle needs a wife, the girls try their best to match up Logan and Sandra. Will these complete opposites discover they were meant to be together?*

**Don't miss**
**TWIN BLESSINGS**
**On sale September 2001**

*Love Inspired*